PRIDE

of the

MOHICANS

PRIDE
of the
MOHICANS

Edited by
VAN ALLEN PLEXICO

WHITE ROCKET BOOKS

This is a work of fiction. All the characters and events portrayed in this book are either products of the author's imagination or are used fictitiously.

Inspired by the novel *The Last of the Mohicans: A Narrative of 1757,* by James Fenimore Cooper

Cover art by Laura Givens
Cover design by Van Allen Plexico

A White Rocket Book
www.whiterocketbooks.com

ISBN-13: 978-0692202357
ISBN-10: 0692202358

First printing: April 2014

0 9 8 7 6 5 4 3 2 1

TABLE OF CONTENTS

INTRODUCTION

It is just prior to the year 1757, and England and France are at war. The bulk of that war is being fought not on the continent of Europe but abroad, among the Asian, African, and American colonies of those two Great Powers. The true victims of the violence are not the soldiers on either side but the common people—both settlers and indigenous peoples—who have found their lives turned upside down by this cataclysm.

As that conflict—which goes by many names, including the Seven Years' War and the Great War for Empire—drags on, it falls to the colonists and the natives alike to choose a side, and perhaps even take up arms themselves, march into the fields, man the defenses, and fight—though their own homes and loved ones possibly be forfeit in the lands they must leave behind. The eventual winner and loser in what would be known in North America as the French and Indian War is of little consequence to most of those people; all that matters to them is preserving their properties, defending their families—and staying alive.

Into this maelstrom of blood and fire come three men; a family comprised of a father and his two sons. They are led by Chingachgook, also called John Mohegan and *Le Gros Serpent*, the wise father who understands the winding and often duplicitous nature of men and is renowned for his ability to strike swiftly, like a snake. The older son—born Nathaniel Poe but also going by the names *La Longue Carabine* and Hawkeye, among others—was adopted by Chingachgook at an early age and is absolute master of the Kentucky Long Rifle. The younger son, Uncas, is a brave and impetuous fighter; his father fears that he is destined to be the last of the Mohican peoples.

These three brave fighters, as drawn from James Fenimore Cooper's novels and Michael Mann's 1992 motion picture, among other depictions, have thrilled and inspired generations of readers and moviegoers with their exploits in defense of freedom and justice. Now four of the finest writers in the New Pulp and Adventure Fiction communities—Jim Beard, Ron Fortier, Frank Schildiner, and I.A. Watson—have come together to give us four glimpses into their lives and adventures in the months prior to their journey to Fort William Henry and their fateful meeting with Cora, Alice, and Colonel Munro; well before the events of the story called *The Last of the Mohicans*.

So join us now, if you will, in the second year of the war between England and France for possession of North America, and watch as three men—the last of a vanishing people—roam the frontier west of the Hudson…

From Within

Jim Beard

1. Separated

He was up a tree and he did not care for it. Not at that moment, anyway.

The man called Hawkeye loved to climb trees when he was a child, loved immersing himself in nature, but he had grown used to the feel of the dirt and the moss and stone beneath his feet as the years progressed. Now, by necessity, he returned to the branches of the sentinels of the great forest but longed to once again plant himself on solid ground.

The view from high up in the great, old tree afforded him an expanse of his surroundings, a view which might lead him to his father and his brother. The two people he loved most in his world had been taken from him and he meant to find them; if that meant climbing a tree and perching on one of its branches like an owl or a squirrel, so be it.

Hawkeye's keen eyes surveyed the scene spread out before him. There, in a clearing in the forest, squatted a collection of human beings who, up until half a day ago, he had no quarrel with. Now, if he could prove that his father and brother were among them and not by choice, he was likely to start an argument with them.

It was a camp he saw there, made up of some three-hundred or more men, if his counting was sound. More than half of them were soldiers or militiamen, while the rest of the assortment was made up of native braves. Hawkeye didn't care for the gathering as much as he didn't care for being up a tree; there was a bad feeling around it all.

He scanned the outskirts of the encampment, then sought out its innards and dissected the entire clump of humanity piece by piece with his eyes. He could not see his family. Underneath his breath, he swore in the Mohawk language.

"Hawkeye!"

The voice called out from below him, near the thick base of the old tree. He looked down into the sun-darkened, sweaty face of a man done up in furs from his head to his toes, including the ring-tailed cap on his head. The man's eyes were as wide as saucers and his lips worked back in forth in consternation.

"Quiet, Jean Regisser," Hawkeye admonished him, waving him back into the shadows.

The man stood his ground and grimaced. His teeth were bad, with many of them missing, in fact.

"Do you see anything?" hissed the man in English that had been thoroughly dipped in a broad French accent. "Can you see Uncas and his *pere*?"

"No," replied the hunter of the forest who did not like being in a tree. "I cannot. It's as if they have disappeared completely."

"That's-that's not good," replied Jean Regisser.

Hawkeye nodded more to himself than anybody.

"No, it's not."

They had been hunting together only the day before; Nathaniel, his brother Uncas, and their father Chingachgook. Moving through the forest along the great river, they kept a distance between themselves and the settlements, as was their custom. The two natives and the white man who ran as a pack of three and three only were not often welcome among others, both white men and red.

The hunting was not good. March had brought cold winds and snow, and the creatures of the forest seemed not to care to show their faces out in the open. After several days of sparse success, Nathaniel, whom some referred to as Hawkeye for his unerring aim with a long rifle, suggested they move southward.

It was then that they crossed paths with an Indian hunting party.

Where Nathaniel and his father and his brother were adept at walking lightly and stealthily, somehow the braves they encountered were better. They numbered twenty and before the three travelers knew what had happened, they were surrounded.

Nathaniel raised his rifle, ready to fight, but Chingachgook urged his white son to wait and allow him to parlay with the braves.

Uncas did not like the situation. While he had great faith in his father to soothe even the most fearsome of beasts, the braves had a strange look about them, one that troubled him.

The warriors appeared of several tribes, none of them Iroquois, the dominant people in the area. Chingachgook spoke to them first in Mohawk, his own tongue, and when that did not bring a response, he made his salutations in Algonkin, a language he was not fluent in, but passable.

"Why do keep us from our path, my brothers?" he asked, his hands empty and spread out before him. "The forest calls to us to continue our hunt."

One brave stepped forward and addressed the older man. He wore both buckskin and European cloth, as well as a big gold ring in his nose. In his hands he held a rifle and at his belt hung a hatchet.

"Why do you travel with this white man, old father?"

Chingachgook smiled, indicated Nathaniel. "This is my son. I call him my own as I do this one." He gestured to Uncas then.

The brave looked all three men up and down, then smiled a toothy smile.

"You will come with us," he said, and then began to turn away.

"We do not wish to, my brother," replied Hawkeye's father. "We will be on our way in peace."

The brave whirled back around at the words, his face livid. "You will come with us!" he bellowed. "You will join with our French fathers as we have done!"

Nathaniel raised his rifle again, seeing which way the wind blew, but he was clubbed savagely clubbed from behind before he could squeeze his trigger.

The last thing he heard was Uncas give a cry of alarm, but before he could return that cry, the braves fell about him, beating at him with their clubs.

The entire world went dark.

He awoke some time later, though how long exactly he was not sure. Fortune smiled on Nathaniel though, for he easily picked up Chingachgook and Uncas' trail – and that trail was not very old.

It took him three hours to catch up to the party; Hawkeye knew how to travel swiftly through the forest, especially when there was prey to catch.

It was then that he saw the soldiers.

A long phalanx of them stretched along a path through the trees, trailed by a band of natives. Nathaniel saw the colors of the French army and he wondered at what brought them together with the Indians.

Reaching a ridge high above the path, he peered down at the troops but could not see his father and brother. His vantage point was not good one and his line of sight was somewhat obscured, but he felt that he'd pierced his target and that he could still help his loved ones.

When the column of soldiers and native warriors stopped to make camp, Nathaniel had arrived upon a plan. He needed to parlay with the French to free Chingachgook and Uncas, but to do that he needed to be able to talk with the soldiers, for he did not speak their language.

Taking one last look at the encampment from afar, he turned and ran off into the forest.

"*S'il vous plaît*, tell me again why I am here, Hawkeye?"

He looked down from his perch once more at the trapper. He did not know the man well, but he knew him well enough, he reasoned. Nathaniel hoped it was not a foolish thing to have brought Jean Regisser into the situation.

"To talk to these soldiers for me," he replied. "I cannot speak French."

The trapper nodded, pulled at his scraggly beard. "Ah, *oui, oui.* I remember now. When is that to be?"

"Soon," came the answer from up above. "For now, let me think."

Nathaniel knew the Iroquois would not be happy over the incursion of other tribes on their lands. That was of no surprise, for they were always fighting with somebody. Chingachgook once said to him that the Iroquois had a "spirit of constant struggle" that hung over them, and for that they were destined to always be at war.

He wondered why the tribes that accompanied the French would dare to do so, knowing they risked war with the Iroquois. And where were they headed and for what purpose?

A grumble issued from below him and he felt sorry that he had dragged the trapper from his cabin several miles away, made him run all the way to the soldiers' camp and then made him wait. It was time to parlay with the French.

On a whim, he cupped his hands around his mouth and gave a call that sounded like that of a hawk. His father and brother should recognize it as his sign to them that he was near.

When no reply came, he dropped out of the tree to the ground and gathered up his rifle and Jean Regisser. Together, they walked back into the forest and began to make a wide arc of a trail to the soldiers' front door.

Nathaniel was not optimistic about their chances, but he had little else to work with.

Soon, they approached the camp along the same path that the phalanx had used earlier. When the sentry who stood in the middle of the path saw Nathaniel and Regisser coming near, he called out in French for them to halt and identify themselves.

"Tell him we are here to speak with his commander on a very grave matter," Nathaniel said to his companion.

The trapper pulled his cap off and, holding it in his hands, stepped closer to the solider and relayed the message. Suddenly, four braves appeared, two one each side of the sentry, menacing in their silence and glowering looks.

Nathaniel resisted the urge to swing his long rifle into a position to fire, and instead radiated what he hoped was an aura of goodwill and peace.

The sentry barked something over his shoulder to another soldier nearby and within a minute a ranking officer walked out from a tent that sat not too far off and approached the scene. He asked something of Regisser in French and the trapper nodded and replied, also in French.

"It seems we are to be taken before their leader," said Regisser to Nathaniel. "*Mon Dieux*, I must be crazy."

"Remain calm, old man," he told the trapper, "and relay everything I tell you to. We *will* walk away from this."

Regisser wrung his cap and frowned. "Yes, but with what missing, *mon ami*?"

They were delivered to the French commander, who introduced himself as Captain Gaspard-Joseph Chaussegros de Léry. Then, he asked what he might be able to do for his visitors…within reason, of course.

Nathaniel instructed the trapper to translate as he talked, and to also translate what de Léry said in reply.

"I was hunting in the woods near here," he said, "with my father and my brother, two Mohicans. We met with a group of your warriors and they press-ganged my family members into their service – *your* service, perhaps."

Pausing to allow Regisser to finish and wait for any comments from the French lieutenant, he continued when none came.

"We have no argument, no quarrel with you or your men, or the braves who attacked me and took my father and brother. We wish only to continue on our way and to leave you to yours."

De Léry listened to the translation and raised one eyebrow. He was a powdered and bewigged thing, but Nathaniel could see that he was not a man to be trifled with.

"I am not aware of my Indian brothers, as you say, 'press-ganging' anyone," he said with a clear, musical voice through the translation of the trapper. "I welcome new native recruits to my forces, assuredly, but would frown upon any such activity as you describe, good sir. Are you certain that they did not go along willingly?"

The question angered the young man called Hawkeye. The thought that Chingachgook and Uncas would choose to go along with a war party was...but, no, he thought to himself; the lieutenant did not know the men, nor what they would or would not do.

He told Regisser to reply in the very strongest negative.

It was clear that once he heard the reply, de Léry was quite dubious about the entire situation.

"Call your warriors here, then," said Nathaniel, "and ask them yourself. If they are honorable men, they will tell the truth of the matter."

The captain smiled, seemingly amused by his guests. Leaning over to a subordinate, the man issued a command in French and swung his eyes back to Nathaniel. He looked him up and down, taking in Hawkeye's garb and the tattoos along his arms. He also studied the Kentucky long rifle that his guest cradled in his arms like a small, precious child.

Into the tent in which they stood strutted a group of braves, the very same ones that had taken Chingachgook and Uncas. The leader said something in French to the lieutenant and the officer replied, casting a pointed finger languidly at Nathaniel and Jean Regisser.

"Our host says that you have a disagreement with the Indian here," the trapper whispered to his companion. "He's also asking him if he took something of yours."

The Iroquois warrior's eyes bored into Nathaniel. Stepping closer to him, he placed his hands on his hips and then shook his head from side to side.

"*Non, non*," said the Indian. He emphasized this with a slashing motion of his hand.

De Léry looked back and forth from his warriors to his guests. "You see there? They know nothing of your…family? I believe you are sadly mistaken about the entire matter, sir."

With that, Nathaniel gave a nod of his head, reached out and grabbed Regisser's shoulder and led him back out of the tent.

"We must leave here," he said to the trapper, calm and collected, "and quickly."

When they had passed the sentry and made their way to the edge of the forest around the clearing, a shot rang out from behind them and something slapped a tree with a loud crack only inches from Nathaniel's head.

"Run!" he yelled.

2. Brother versus Brother

The trees welcomed the hunted as they slipped between them and away from the hunters. Twenty paces in, Nathaniel saw the trapper suddenly plunge to the ground and burrow beneath the dead leaves and the snow there. In the blink of an eye, he was gone.

Loading his rifle, Nathaniel turned to fight.

An Indian brave rushed headlong at him, but fell when he pulled the trigger to discharge his rifle. Then, letting the weapon fall to the ground, he took out his hatchet and steeled himself for the next attack.

It came within seconds. Two braves screeched like angry owls as they sailed through air at him. He sidestepped the one and caught him in the back of the neck with the sharp blade of his hatchet, nearly severing the spine. Pulling the hatchet free, Nathaniel spun around and countered a blow from the other brave. The shock of the impact from the two weapons reverberated through his arm, almost making him drop his hatchet.

Nathaniel leapt forward, catching his opponent in the lower abdomen with his knee. Air exploded from the man's lungs and he brought the hatchet swinging upward to catch the Indian in the throat. Blood sprayed in a fine mist from the gaping wound.

Panting from the fighting, he whirled around to face whatever danger might come next.

Two more Indians appeared from between the trees and Nathaniel raised his hatchet, ready for the onslaught.

The two approached him and he recognized the faces of his father and his brother.

"We are not alone!" said Chingachgook, concern etched into his weathered countenance. "We were made to go with the hunting party, my son…"

Cries split the air and echoed among the trees. Uncas looked back over his shoulder, then to Nathaniel. He pushed his father out of the way and raised his hatchet above his head.

"Defend yourself!" he hissed, and attacked.

Hawkeye was bewildered for a split second, but raised his own weapon and caught Uncas' first blow with a defensive action. Indian braves exploded onto the scene and he realized his brother's scheme.

They were to make it look good.

Chingachgook placed himself between Uncas and the others, calling out to them.

"Do not interfere! My son has challenged the white intruder! Allow them the honor of the fight!"

Circling each other, the two brothers, one white and one red, looked into each others' eyes and silently made their intentions known. They moved in and the battle was joined.

Uncas and Nathaniel had fought many times, but never in anger or in fear. They had tested each other for years, honing their skills in mock combat, all the time under the watchful eye of Chingachgook. In this manner, they had become accomplished warriors.

Both men remained silent as they battled, releasing only grunts as they searched for weaknesses in each other's defenses. To their audience there in the forest, they appeared to be in a fight to the death, but in reality it was simply another exercise for them. But they made it look good.

Nathaniel came in swinging his hatchet, every swipe of the deadly blade pressing Uncas backwards. If he guessed his brother's plan accurately, he needed to make himself look brash and somewhat reckless. Uncas avoided each blow, his face serious and composed. Then, seeing an opening, he went on the offensive and kicked out with one leg, sending his brother sprawling backwards.

Around him, the braves laughed and whooped; they were enjoying the contest.

Chingachgook knew to not allow fear for his sons to wash over him. He knew to trust them both that the path they chose was the right one and that the means to an end were worthwhile. That said, he silently wished they did not have to make it look so good.

Nathaniel came down hard on top of the body of the brave he had caught in the throat. Slipping in the man's blood, he righted himself and felt around for his hatchet. Behind him, Uncas stepped up, ready to continue the fight.

One of the braves called out for Uncas to finish off the white man, that he was a coward if he did not end the battle immediately. Nathaniel heard the jibe and grinned to himself;

the man really did not know his brother, one of the bravest men he'd ever known, in the slightest.

He jumped to his feet and turned to face Uncas, hatchet in hand once more.

Uncas came in low and swung his own weapon in a wide arc on an upward angle. Hawkeye screeched as the blade whistled past his face and then gurgled as he clutched at his throat.

Blood oozed from between his fingers and his eyes went wide in horror. He let his hands fall away to reveal a throat covered in a mass of blood, with small pieces of it dropping away from the wound.

Nathaniel's eyes rolled up into his head and he fell backwards, hitting a tree and flopping face first into the cold snow and mud that covered the ground. His feet and hands twitched once, twice, three times, and then were still.

One of the Indian braves stepped forward and moved as to check the body, perhaps even to take its scalp. Uncas bellowed at the man.

"Leave him! He is nothing! Let him lie in the mud as nothing!"

With that he spat on the body and turned on his heel to stalk away. Chingachgook eyed the braves soberly and then followed after his son.

The Indians looked at each other and turned to leave.

"They are gone now, *mon ami*. You can return from *la mort*."

Nathaniel opened his eyes one by one. The forest was relatively silent around him, save for the course voice of Jean Regisser.

The man was covered with dirt and leaves, but smiling and obviously happy to be alive. He offered a wineskin to the younger man, and when it was refused, drank thoroughly from it himself.

"What now, Nathaniel?" asked Regisser, hoping his part was done.

Hawkeye considered this for a quiet moment while he wiped away the blood and gore he'd taken from the body of the brave he killed. With it, he had fooled his attackers into thinking Uncas had won. His brother had filled his role as victor well; now, he needed to find Chingachgook and Uncas again and free them from their bondage.

"I'm going after them."

The trapper got up and looked around. "You are welcome to it, *mon brave*," he announced. "For me, I return to my cabin and my solitude. *Bon voyage...*"

Nathaniel wished him well, thanked him for his aid and watched him as disappeared into the forest. Then he picked up his rifle and hatchet, shook his head ruefully at the carnage arrayed around him and walked off in the direction of his family.

Finding a suitable spot away from the main road, he then hunkered down to wait for nightfall to be complete.

Nathaniel moved again not long before daybreak. Flexing his muscles and massaging his limbs to shake off the cold that had seeped into them, he found his way through the forest and skirted along the edges of the French camp.

There he saw clearly the signs of not only the regular French soldiers and their Indian partners, but also men he'd heard the English call bush lopers. Mostly Canadians, they stood as fighters to rival the native braves; stories told around campfires painted the lopers as men who'd do anything an Indian would, including the eating of their enemies' flesh.

Nathaniel wondered again what set the entire oddly-formed army on their path. It could only mean trouble for someone, most likely the British.

He had no special love for the British or the French. He and his father and brother wanted simply to live their lives and go where they wished, unobstructed by white or red man. For the most part, they'd been able to do just that, but recently the air had changed and the old paths had grown dark with the increasing number of skirmishes between the land's prospective new tenants.

Once more, he cupped his hands around his mouth and let loose with the cry of a hawk. Holding his breath, he strained his ears for a response.

This time it came. Chingachgook and Uncas had heard him.

Nathaniel got up and stretched his legs. Then, he began to walk around the borders of the encampment, keeping one eye out for sentries and one for his father and brother. Periodically, he gave out with the hawk's cry.

Pausing behind a large grouping of boulders that squatted upon a small rise near the camp, he decided it would make a good meeting place. Crying out once more in the hawk's voice, he climbed upon the largest of the boulders and lay flat in the thin covering of frost along its nearly level top.

Within twenty minutes, two figures approached his position from the camp.

One of the men called out his name.

"Here," he called back and then slid down off the rock to the side of it that faced away from the soldiers.

Both Chingachgook and Uncas reached out to clasp wrists, arms and shoulders with him, though they did not smile as they did so. Nathaniel knew the seriousness of the situation.

"Why did they take you?" he asked his father, looking him over for signs of abuse from either the French or his fellow natives.

Chingachgook spread his hands wide. "They want to increase their numbers, to help the French in their task."

"Which is?" Nathaniel asked.

"We have made it clear that we wish to know this," replied Uncas, "but the tongues of our brothers in this band are not loose. All we can determine is that we head toward a fort. A British fort."

Hawkeye digested that, then spoke again.

"The nearest such fort is Williams, on the Mohawk," he noted, "but that is too well fortified for this group. They can't be seriously considering attacking it."

Both Chingachgook and Uncas nodded in agreement. "They have cannon there, too, at Williams," added Uncas.

"That leaves the other in the area, on the other end of the Great Carrying Place," said Nathaniel. "I do not know what name it's called."

Chingachgook spoke. "I have heard it called Wood Creek, after the waterway it sits upon, not far from the lake called Oneida. But I too have heard it named Bull, for the British man who sits there."

"Who are these braves who have joined with the French on this path?" Nathaniel inquired, truly curious. He looked from his brother to his father and back again.

"Caughnawagas, mostly," answered Chingachgook. "Also Algonkins and Nipissings."

"I asked of one brave why he would follow the French to war," said Uncas. "He said only that his home and his family were under the wrath of the soldiers if he and his brothers did not join in with them."

Hawkeye nodded. "That may explain why they would in turn risk the wrath of the Iroquois for making war on their lands."

When his father and brother fell silent, he pressed them further.

"You cannot stay here among them," Nathaniel urged, pointing toward the encampment. "Come, let's go and not look back. Leave them to their own destruction."

His father reached out and placed his hand at the back of his neck, cupping his head and holding it firmly.

"No, my son. Uncas and I will stay. *You* must go."

Without saying a word in response to Chingachgook's statement, Nathaniel illustrated his confusion with his eyes.

"Our brothers here are not happy, not content," said the older man. "They walk along the *edge* of the path, one foot in darkness, the other in light. They can be brought fully into the light and away from the path of the French. This I know in my heart."

Hawkeye skewered Uncas with a piercing look.

"You agree with this?" he asked his brother.

Uncas nodded, frowned. "Yes. I have seen it too. The braves are distrustful of the soldiers and are not sure if they are being lied to about their homes and families. But, they are also eager to fight and strike blows against the white man – no matter what side their hatchets fall upon."

Chingachgook spread his hands again. "We must work from within, Nathaniel. Given a chance, we will try to lead them away from the fight that is surely coming. From the innocent blood they will shed."

Hawkeye was overwhelmed by the wisdom of his father. He could find no argument of merit to give, save that the two would be placing themselves in danger should they stay.

"Go then," he said, "stay and fight from within. But I will not *leave you*. I will shadow you to the bitter end, father."

All three men clasped hands again, affirming their bonds to each other.

"We must return to the camp," Uncas insisted, "before we are missed."

Nathaniel was about to agree with him, but a loud cry issued forth from the encampment and a thrill of alarm shot through him.

"Your absence has been discovered!" he hissed, looking all around them.

Chingachgook stood up, listening.

"No," he said soothingly. "But with the dawn comes a new problem. They have captured someone."

Nathaniel watched from a safe vantage point as the camp roused itself and became aware of recent events.

Down the road came three wagons surrounded by Indians and Canadian bush lopers. The wagons were brought to a stop and twelve men in all were forced from to come down from them. The men wore the uniforms of the British army.

The Indians sneered and whooped, proud of the capture. De Léry himself came out to survey the prisoners and then ordered the men bound and made to sit on the ground while the camp uprooted itself and made to travel once more.

Hawkeye also saw his father turn toward his hiding spot and nod slightly. Then, Chingachgook and Uncas made their way over to their fellow natives and helped to pack away tents and other supplies.

He watched for a few minutes more. Now, he had others to free as well as his loved ones.

It would take some doing.

3. A Rescue

Chingachgook strode up to one of the braves he'd talked with before and asked him to step to one side for talk. The man looked around suspiciously, then nodded his agreement.

"We move to war," said the older man, plainly stating the situation. His tone was level, his entire being calm and reserved.

"Yes," replied the brave. "Our French father will most likely question the men we have captured. Then, we will go to fight."

"Is this what you want, what you desire?" asked Chingachgook.

The brave blinked, then looked away from the older man. Chingachgook saw the uncertainty present in him, but remained outwardly at peace and did not show the anxiety he felt.

"You are far from your home," he continued, "far from your family. It is not wrong to think of them first, instead of the French. You have a duty to your family – I do not see the duty you believe you owe to these men around us."

The brave closed his eyes, held them tightly shut, as if by doing so he could make the words that had been spoken go away.

"We *must* see this through," he hissed through clenched teeth. "The soldiers tell us that-that our lands will be *burned* and that our families will be made to *suffer*..."

Chingachgook reached out and placed his hand on the younger man's shoulder. He felt the muscles there flinch, but the brave did not shrug it off or move away.

"You are a leader among your people here. Your voice is strong. They will listen to you. We go to the slaughter, not to victory. The French father has blood in his eyes, but not just the blood of his enemies, the British. He has *our* blood there, too."

Chingachgook paused, watching for the effects of his words on the brave.

"And he does not care if he spills it."

A long silence passed between the two men, and then, finally, the younger of them spoke.

"What can we *do*?"

The older man did not smile, though the urge was strong. "We can follow our hearts and leave this place. Return to our families. Mine waits for me, too. Out there."

The brave opened his eyes and looked into Chingachgook's.

"I will consider it."

Once again lying prone on the top of the big rock, Nathaniel viewed the camp. More specifically, he watched the British prisoners.

While his men made ready to travel again, Captain de Léry returned to stand in front of the bound soldiers. One of the British stood when the Frenchman stopped in front of them and the two men began to converse.

Even at far range, Nathaniel could see the difficulty de Léry was having with the conversation; most likely the man's English was not good. Regardless, it was the sort of polite exchange that usually transpired between military opponents and that always amused him to a degree.

The world could be falling apart all around them, but decorum must always be maintained.

After a minute or so, the French captain made a curt bow and, swiveling on his heels, walked away from his prisoners. The British soldier sat back down and leaned in to talk with his companions.

Nathaniel had a very bad feeling about it all.

Though the cold of the rock was seeping into his bones, he made up his mind to wait a bit more and see what might present itself. Within an hour, the scene abruptly changed.

A small band of Indian, ten in all, marched over to the prisoners and, through gestures, forced the men to stand. A few of the braves then stepped behind the soldiers and cut their bonds, freeing the men's hands. The relief of being free to massage their arms and increase their circulation was short-lived though. Again, through gestures and perhaps some broken English, the braves issued orders to the British men.

The men refused, vehemently. The barrels of rifles were placed against their heads.

As Nathaniel watched in confusion, the soldiers began to disrobe. Soon, they stood in the bitter cold of the early March morning in only their heavy cotton undergarments. The men's uniforms now sat in piles at their feet.

Some of the Indians gathered up the uniforms and carried them off, while the remaining braves shuffled the British into a line, bound their hands once more, and then pointed off into the forest.

Nathaniel knew that they were being marched off to their deaths.

Thinking quickly, trying to formulate a plan of action, he saw Uncas, his brother, suddenly jog up to the braves and begin to speak to them.

The conversation very rapidly grew animated and then heated. One of the natives raised his arm, holding up a hatchet, and wagged it at Uncas.

Nathaniel's brother's hand shot out and caught the wrist of the brave, holding it in place above their heads. The two stared at each other.

Chingachgook appeared and stepped between the two warriors. The older man spoke for a few seconds, but the collected braves seemed to want none of it. Uncas and Chingachgook were forced to step back and allow the British soldiers to be marched out of the camp.

"It was a good try, my brother," Nathaniel whispered to himself, then prepared himself for what was to come next.

He kept his perch on the large boulder, for he saw that the column of soldiers was being directed into the trees not far from his spot. Silently, he began to lay out his powder and his ammunition next to him on the rock.

Having loaded his rifle in the swift, expert way that was his fashion, the man known as Hawkeye turned himself fully around to face the other direction and settled the long weapon in his hands. Then, he watched and waited.

In a small clearing some one-hundred yards from his position, the native braves halted the line of British men and had them stand facing away from the camp. Nathaniel gave all credit to the soldiers; for the most part, they held themselves up well in the face of what they had to know was transpiring. He could see them shivering, but only one of the men showed signs of weakness. That one sobbed quietly, but still stood in his place.

The braves, six of them now, arrayed themselves behind the twelve men, so as to be between them and Hawkeye. One of the Indians walked down the line in front of the soldiers, eyeing each one of them in turn but saying nothing. At the end of the row, he stopped and looked at his fellows.

Nathaniel sighted down the long barrel of his rifle. He'd have but one shot at it, possibly two, with no goodly amount of time to reload. Still, he prepared to do so before he'd be forced to bring the fight directly to the native warriors.

But where to place his shot? The question hung over him like a lead weight.

The answer came like lightning. The lead brave nodded to the others and they all stepped up to the soldiers they stood behind and raised their knives. One of the Indians was quicker about it than his brothers.

Hawkeye pulled the trigger. A crimson cloud obscured the head of the brave. The body sagged and fell.

Five sets of native eyes turned to him - or in his general direction, at least. Five sets of eyes narrowed and scanned his position. Five mouths opened to screech outrage and warning.

He reloaded in record time, pulled the trigger. The ball went through the neck of one brave and out the other side. That body pitched backwards and into a British soldier, knocking the man to the cold ground.

Nathaniel released his rifle and slid down off the boulder. With hatchet in hand, he ran hunched over yet swift as an elk toward his targets.

The first brave that came at him he downed with one quick swipe of his weapon. The second was even clumsier and fell easily.

The third sported two hatchets and these the brave swung in deadly arcs, around and around in front of him. Nathaniel whooped and dodged the first swing that came near him. The move brought him low to the ground and he kicked out with one foot at the legs of his opponent. So focused was the Indian on his hatchet work that he neglected any attack from below – he tumbled and fell upon his own blades.

Nathaniel sprung up and at the fourth brave, but mentally reminded himself that there was a total of two remaining.

He swung his hatchet but the blow was expertly deflected by the brave. His finger involuntarily spasmed from the impact and opened, releasing the weapon to the wind. His opponent moved into the opening he spied and swung his blade at Hawkeye's midsection.

A sharp pain in his gut made him wince, but Nathaniel gritted his teeth and punched at the man with a closed fist. This connected with the brave's bony jaw and snapped his head back. With absolutely no hesitation, he swung his other fist into the brave's belly and received a loud, satisfying grunt of discomfort as reward.

He then brought his knee up into the Indian's jaw, caught the hatchet that was slipping from his grip and sliced the sun-baked throat that was presented to him.

Breathing hard, Nathaniel braced himself for the sixth and last brave.

When no attack came, he opened his eyes wide to see a lone British soldier standing over the Indian in question with a bloody knife clutched in hands that were still bound. In the dirt below him, his would-be killer's blood oozed out and mixed with the frost and scant flora.

The soldier looked up at Hawkeye with a wary eye.

"I'm not your enemy."

The soldier shivered and nodded slowly at the words, as if they were taking then long route to penetrate his brain.

"Aye," he said, finally. "I can see that now. You have my thanks, sir."

Nathaniel scooped up a fallen knife and motioned for the man to hold out his hands. After cutting the leather ties that bound them, he looked up and waved for the other soldiers to approach him. They did so eagerly, but each one of them watched their savior with a hint of suspicion.

"Corporal Thomas Vine," announced the first soldier, "in His Majesty's service. How came you to be here at this most opportune time, sir?"

Nathaniel walked to each fallen native to verify that they were all truly dead. As he did this, he also collected all the hatchets and knives.

"Saw as you were brought into the camp," he told Vine. "My father and brother have been pressed into the French's service. I aim to free them before they can get into any mischief. That's my only concern."

"And yet you bothered to save us."

Going around the circle of men and holding out weapons for them to take, he glanced back only fleetingly at the corporal.

"I have no great admiration or affection for the British," he said plainly, "nor for the French, either. I just don't like to see a slaughter if I don't have to. I'm sure you understand."

Vine nodded, took a proffered blade from him. "Indeed," he replied. "And again, I thank you, sir. We would be dead now if it weren't for your timely intervention. How can we repay this debt?"

Nathaniel eyed the man with a steely gaze. "You're from Bull?"

The soldiers all nodded.

"Then," said their benefactor, "you can repay me by making your way to Fort Williams and let them know there's soon going to be trouble at Bull. Lots of it."

Vine shook his head. "That's all well and good, sir, but we're not exactly dressed for such a journey."

Nathaniel looked down at the men's sodden feet, some of them bare and others clad only in woolen socks that had seen better days.

"Then listen to me and listen good," he told them. "I have a friend not far from here. He'll equip you as best he can – but get to Williams as swiftly as you can and *warn them.*"

He barked out brief directions and turned on his heel to stalk off in the direction of the big rock once again.

The British soldiers watched him go for several seconds, then turned to leave the area themselves.

In the empty clearing, a lone native stepped out from behind a big, wide tree and glanced once in the direction of the man he assumed to be a ghost and then toward the soldiers who were supposed to be dead.

He walked off after the soldiers.

By the time he had reached his boulder perch to retrieve his rifle and other belongings, Nathaniel saw the tail end of the French leaving the campsite.

Among those departing, he saw the captured British wagon. In it sat men in dressed in British army uniforms.

He swore under his breath and prayed that Chingachgook and Uncas were still alive and unharmed.

After a moment's consideration on what to do next, he made up his mind and trotted down into the deserted campsite. There, he found one of the firepits used by the soldiers and squatted down over it. Scooping up some of the ash from the pit, he began to smear it over his face and through his hair. Then, he applied the ash to his neck and the backs of his hands.

Checking the wound on his belly, he saw that it was only superficial. With his own blood he drew tears upon his face, weeping of blood from his eyes.

Nathaniel stood up, rearranged the things he carried, and began to march back into the forest.

He looked as he hoped he would: a walking dead man.

4. The Ghost of the Forest

The early morning sun struggled to pierce the clouds that hung over the landscape as the column of soldiers and native braves marched toward Fort Bull. Overall, they passed through a dreary setting, made all the more strange and foreboding by the specter that harried them at every turn.

Within a matter of just a few hours, the braves began to talk among themselves of what was surely the ghost of the white man they had dispatched the day before. They saw it flit between the trees, revealing itself only for a moment before disappearing again. They could hear the sound of its footfalls in the frost and the dried leaves and twigs that littered the ground. Some of the natives claimed they could hear its mocking laughter on the wind.

Others said its skin was grey and ashen, and that it cried blood over its own lost life.

The Canadian bush lopers tried to ignore what the Indians reported until they could take it no longer and wanted to send out a few scouts to capture the "ghost." The French officers on horseback would have none of it and ordered the men to hold the line and stay in formation - they'd be arriving at their destination soon enough.

But even they were unnerved when they passed a tree upon which hung the carcass of a recently killed rabbit, its blood still fresh and its entrails steaming where they hung out from the animal's split belly.

From within the march, Chingachgook and Uncas appraised the situation and saw its advantages. The younger man even spread his own talk through the ranks of his fellow natives, of how he had seen the spirit and knew that it was that of the man he'd killed in the forest. There was no doubt that the spirit was angry and sought vengeance.

Then, the young brave that Chingachgook had been currying favor with approached him, falling in step with the older man, one eye on the forest that seemed to press in around them.

"We are with you," he said, his voice low.

Chingachgook nodded. "How many?"

The brave brought his hands up and flashed ten fingers twice.

"And they are prepared to leave this madness, even if it means they must fight their way out?"

The brave bowed his head in agreement.

"This is wise," pronounced Chingachgook. "We must wait for the right time – there may be even more good we can do if we watch for the opportunity."

"How will we know?" asked the brave, clearly disturbed by the weight of the morning's strangeness and his coming desertion.

The older man offered a slight smile. "Look for my signal. You will know when it comes."

Uncas drifted up beside his father as the young brave returned to his original place in the column.

"Nathaniel is working wonders," he said. "The French father is unhappy, or so the Canadians have learned from the soldiers. What was once unity is splintering into discord, thanks to the ghost of the forest."

"Still, we must be wary of danger," his father replied. "Nathaniel walks a thorny path, as do we. We now have twenty of our brothers who are ready to leave, but I fear it will not be enough to widen the cracks in the wood of this spear."

Uncas pondered this as he walked. He trusted his brother and longed to once again hunt at his side, but he felt what his father felt, too. There were many unseen things that swirled around them, and not just Nathaniel's play-acting.

A murmur arose around them, whispers and then raised voices that announced a new wrinkle in the fabric of their march. The word came back along the line: a prisoner had been taken.

Chingachgook and Uncas looked at each other, worry creasing their brows as the dread of fear for Hawkeye crept into them.

Away from the column of French, Canadians, and Indians, the ghost raised his head among the trees and brush and watched as the march came to a stop. Something had happened.

First he heard shouts in French, which he could not understand, then similar shouts in a native tongue. From those he understood enough to learn that someone had been captured and that the prisoner was being hauled up the line to the French commander.

Hawkeye scanned the ranks of men and caught sight of one of the bush lopers pulling a bound man along.

It was Jean Regisser.

He cursed long and low, looking up to the sky and asking the Great Spirit why it must be so. The man was an innocent, his only crime being the aid he'd given to Nathaniel a day or so ago.

Rifle raised, he sighted down it and drew an invisible line between its barrel and the head of the bush loper who guided the trapper. With one squeeze of the trigger, he'd punish the man who had torn his friend from his home and, in doing so, expose himself to the soldiers and Indians.

A cold breeze wafted over him and cooled the heat of the moment. Nathaniel realized that a shot now would do little good; in fact, it would most likely make matters worse. Things were heading toward a predestined end and he could not afford to lose all – Regisser, his father and brother – with a single, undisciplined action.

He'd wait, though it pained him to remain inactive. He would remain a spirit, haunting the column and watching for the moment of his vengeance to arrive.

Hawkeye arrived at Fort Bull with the soldiers and their native accomplices, but only as their shadow, not as a willing participant.

It was late in the afternoon. The sun still struggled in vain to show itself, casting a deathly pall across the trees and the waterway called Wood Creek. Nathaniel hung back, seeking higher ground to gain a better view of the fort and the land that surrounded it.

He had been through the area before, just two winters ago, but the fort had not existed then. He saw that it was still fairly new, not much more than a year since its construction, but he was not impressed by it. As a stronghold, it left much to be desired.

Fort Bull hunkered down on the south bank of the creek with its walls in the form of a star. From his viewing spot, Nathaniel could see that while the walls themselves looked strong enough and the double row of pointed stakes set close together that ringed them appeared somewhat threatening, they guarded nothing more than a small grouping of storehouses.

He wondered what it was that the British cared to defend there. In all, it seemed laughable, at least to him.

Beyond the fort, on its far side, the Great Carrying Place began, a road of commerce and supplies that ran from Fort Bull to Fort Williams along the Mohawk River. To the east of Bull, Lake Oneida sat, calm and big.

Nathaniel had no idea at all how many people populated the fort, or whether or not there were also women and children in residence. He prayed it was only men of war, those who expected to fight and possibly to die in the doing.

The French line paused some distance from the fort. He could see de Léry striding back and forth, viewing his target through a glass and conferring with his officers. Then, he spat some order and the soldiers parted to allow the wagon to roll up.

Hawkeye suddenly saw their plan materialize before him and he understood it with crystal clarity.

Inside the wagon sat the men of de Léry's who had dressed themselves in British uniforms robbed from their former prisoners – the soldiers he'd sent on their way to Regisser.

The wagon lurched into movement, heading toward the gates of Fort Bull carrying the mock-British soldiers.

Once more he raised his long rifle and sifted through the choices before him, determined to prevent a slaughter.

A disturbance of some kind sprang up among the Indians, such that it caught at his ears and brought his attention. Then, a cry split the air.

He swung his gaze to the wagon; still moving toward the fort, it was only fifty yards from its gate.

Nathaniel smiled. He recognized Uncas' war-cry. The men in the wagon were undone, now forced to make a decision in the wake of their scheme to fool the men in the fort. As he guessed they might, the mock-British hesitated and slowed their horses.

"You'd have done better to have made a run for the gates," he said aloud to the wind, shaking his head. "They might have believed you were chased by braves and let you in…"

Shouts came from behind the walls of the fort; Nathaniel assumed that the ploy had been spotted and now the British were on alert. Looking back to de Léry and his troops, he suddenly heard the wagon moving again and turned to see what was happening.

In horror Hawkeye watched as the men in the wagon leapt out, ran to up to the fort and positioned themselves in front of its portholes. Inserting their rifles through the openings, they opened fire.

Nathaniel screeched his defiance and raised his rifle to shoot one of the men through the heart.

Uncas saw one of the disguised French stagger and fall to the ground and heard the echo of a rifle's report. In his heart, he knew his brother was at work.

Cries went up all around him and hatchets and rifles were raised aloft. He spotted his father and made eye-contact; the older man nodded solemnly and turned to look for those he owed a signal. Uncas, jostled aside by the onrushing phalanx of natives, gripped his own rifle and tried to weigh his options.

A strong hand gripped his shoulder suddenly and he swung around to look into the face of Chingachgook, pride of the Mohicans, a warrior without peer. Behind him gathered twenty braves, all of them possessed of a controlled fury. Uncas nodded to his father and Chingachgook released his small army to their fates.

The Indians rushed out into the clearing around Fort Bull first, followed by the Canadian bush lopers and then finally by the French soldiers. Chingachgook's native deserters pounced on the trailing end of the soldiers and attacked.

Reloading, Nathaniel took aim once more and sent another soldier to his maker. Inside the fort, cries of anguish sprung up as the mock-British continued to fire through the holes in the walls.

Something tickled him at the back of his head, some extra sense that asked for his attention. He turned to see that all of de Léry's troops were now on the field and heading for the palisades and walls of the fort. Near the back of the line, he spied Jean Regisser, still bound and being dragged along by a soldier.

So captured by the sight, Nathaniel stepped out into the open. Captain de Léry, from atop his steed, saw him in an instant.

The French commander shouted out in French to Regisser's guard, who in turn took a step back and ran the trapper through with his bayonet.

Hawkeye could see nothing beyond the dark rope of blood that trailed from Regisser's back to the pointed edge of the bayonet. He saw only the slow-motion crumbling of his friend's legs and his lifeless eyes as they rolled up into his head. There was no sound to it, only the silence of death.

He'd unconsciously reloaded his rifle and scarce realized it as he brought it up and put a ball between the soldier's own uncaring eyes.

All of a sudden, sounds rushed back into his perception and the battle seemed to arise from the ground around him and engulf him.

A man's voice came to his ears, shouting something. He looked up to see a French officer on horseback, waving a sword and yelling "*Vous rendre! Posez vos armes!*" A strange quiet fell over the entire scene and many faces glanced at the gates of Fort Bull in anticipation.

Without hesitation, the call was answered from inside the walls: "Never!"

De Léry grimaced in his saddle and barked out another command. A group of bush lopers ran toward the gates sporting big axes. When the reached their target, they began to chop at the wood of the gates, hacking away pieces of it with every swing. French soldiers unleashed more ammunition through the fort's portholes, as a deterrent to those who might interfere with the axmen.

Nathaniel looked on numbly, unable to rouse himself into action. It seemed as if it would transpire despite his lack of agreement. He wondered where his father and brother were, but suspected – no, *knew* – they'd be in the thick of it all. He wished he could find them.

Within moments, the gate of Fort Bull came crashing down under the axes and once more Captain de Léry demanded the occupants surrender.

Once more came the refusal.

With thunderous cries of "*Vive le Roi!*" the French swept into the fort with their Indian confederates shouting their own declarations of war at their side.

5. The Battle of Fort Bull

With his great ax smeared with French blood, Chingachgook took a step backwards, then another. In the face of overwhelming opposition, he and the few deserters who still clung to life were forced to retreat.

Across the clearing from the relative-safety of the surrounding trees, the warrior saw the fort under heavy siege and he closed his eyes in shame to it.

Uncas, his son, came to his side and placed a reassuring hand on his arm.

"We are not to blame."

Chingachgook looked at him, saw the wisdom in Uncas' eyes; he was proud of the man he'd become.

"No, we are not," said the older man, "but still I hear the spirits of the dead and cannot close my ears to them. I thought we could save more."

Uncas tightened his grip on his father's arm. "We have saved *these* brothers, and that must be enough."

Chingachgook turned to the half-dozen braves who still followed him and nodded.

"Come, my brothers," he said to them, rising up to his full height. "Let us find my other son, the ghost of the forest, and see what we can see..."

They found Nathaniel standing among a few dead soldiers in the field outside the fort, some one-hundred yards or more from its smashed gates. The young man stood there, cradling his long rifle, as if one of the dead had gotten to his feet and wondered what he should do next.

Uncas asked what in the world he'd done to his face.

Together, they watched as the Indians in the fort cut down the last of its occupants and the French allowed them their carnage. It appeared as if the natives poured out all their anger, all their frustrations at the encroachment of the white man across their lands into the walls of the stockade for it to take root there. It did not last long but it was more slaughter than Nathaniel and his father and his brother had seen in a long while.

With a word from the nervous braves who shuffled around behind them, the three men removed themselves to a safer place among the great trees and turned once more to watch and to mourn.

Captain de Léry surveyed the action, looking calm and satisfied. He'd gotten what he wanted, Nathaniel surmised; the destruction of a British stronghold, a bit of chaos with which to poke his enemies the British in their collective eye.

It was no wonder he sat serenely in his saddle – no doubt he imagined the praise he'd receive back at the French headquarters up the St. Lawrence.

A tall Indian approached the man, hands bloodied and slipping his stained hatchet from hand to hand. French officer and native conversed momentarily and then the brave spun on his heel and loped back to his fellows. There, he yipped and yelped at them, raising his hands and then bringing his weapon down in one great slashing motion.

The Indians ran about, beginning to take scalps. De Léry turned his horse and looked the other way.

Hawkeye raised his rifle and began to load it.

"No," said Chingachgook, firmly but not unkindly. "It would not matter. The wheel would continue to turn and perhaps without us on it. Let us leave this place, Nathaniel, and wash the blood from our hands."

It took him several minutes to reflect upon his father's words, and when he was ready to turn his face from the carnage, Uncas held up a hand and urged them all to look to where he was pointing.

A single file line of French soldiers marched away from one of the big storehouses within the fort under the direction of a few of the officers. On their backs, each one of them carried a large sack. A few of them worked with rolling an immense barrel away from the building.

"What is that?" asked Uncas.

Hawkeye studied the action, then spoke. "Gunpowder. De Léry must have discovered it was being stored here, from when he talked to his British prisoners at the camp. The fort is a stockpile for it."

He looked down for a moment, deep in thought. Then he glanced over at his father and brother.

"You are thinking the same thing that I am thinking."

The two men both nodded grimly.

Surprisingly, one of the Indian braves stepped forward and asked to be told what was happening. When Uncas explained, the native smiled.

"Let *us* light the fire then," he said.

Obviously, there was more powder stored at Fort Bull then the French could ever hope to carry away. They had only the one wagon and that was soon full to a breaking point to be loaded further. The captain ordered his men to begin to form into lines for departure.

At their vantage point, Nathaniel watched as three of his father's deserters crept along through the brush and then up over the wall of the fort.

Interestingly, de Léry ordered his own fires to be set.

"He intends to burn the place to the ground," observed Nathaniel. "But see how he directs his men to torch areas far from the powder he leaves behind?"

"He is wise in that," Chingachgook offered, "for he may put distance between himself and his handiwork before the fire reaches the powder."

The three men said no more, but waited and watched. This was made all the more difficult by the sight of the corpses that littered the dirt around the fort.

Finally, Hawkeye's heart surged as he saw the three braves slip back over the wall and make their way back to their spot. Chingachgook pointed to the gates. There, the French soldiers and Indians were just exiting.

The explosion nearly knocked them all to the ground.

Staggered, Nathaniel looked to see that his father and brother were all right, then peered through the black smoke and bright flames to see the soldiers trying to put themselves back together.

De Léry had been thrown from his horse. A lower officer was running to catch the beast and bring it back.

Another explosion, smaller this time, sent the French and Indians scrambling farther away from Fort Bull, their eyes wide with shock and fear. Nathaniel's mouth stretched into a tight line; part of him wanted to yell with joy, but the overwhelming loss of life would not permit him the luxury.

The French captain shouted at his men, berating them soundly. Then, having regained his mount, he whipped the animal into a gallop that sped him away from the fiery destruction. His army followed, abandoning the wagon laden with gunpowder.

"That will be loud enough to be heard at Fort Williams," noted Uncas.

"We can only hope," replied Nathaniel.

They decided to stay in the area until the next day, to see who might arrive to help, though the fort and its inhabitants were far beyond that.

The six native braves made their exit at dawn. To Chingachgook and Uncas they made their farewells, but looked upon Nathaniel with unease and perhaps even mistrust.

Around noon, as the sun reached its apex and finally broke through the dark clouds, men arrived at the ruins of the fort. Nathaniel saw that they were militia and Iroquois, led by a British officer whose commanding presence was in strong evidence.

Cautioning his father and brother to stay behind and out of sight, he went down to greet the men.

When he appeared out of the forest, the militiamen were startled at first, but a few of them seemed to recognize

Nathaniel. The Indians stared dully at him, keeping their own counsel.

He took himself over to the officer and offered explanations of what they would find in the smoldering fort.

"I am Sir William Johnson," said the man, "recently appointed Superintendent of Indian Affairs for these northern colonies. And you are, sir?"

"Nathaniel Poe, a traveler of these 'northern colonies'."

Johnson narrowed his eyes. "I believe I may know of you, but I also believe I detect a hint of derision in your tone, sir, when you say that."

"A discussion for another time," said Nathaniel, waving it off. "You've got far more trouble *here* than worrying over my likes and dislikes."

And he began to tell the tale of Fort Bull.

"The French father's braves left messages on the trees," said Chingachgook to his white son. "For the Iroquois."

Nathaniel nodded. "Johnson's men don't like it. The Iroquois are angered that other tribes would make war on their lands. It'll lead to no good, that's for certain."

"Where do we go now?" asked Uncas, joining them. He turned to look at the still-smoking ruins of the fort, at the graves that were being dug for the men who had perished there.

"South?" asked Hawkeye. "Maybe to Kain-tuck-ee? Anywhere that takes us from *here*, I reckon."

Chingachgook did not disagree, but simply bowed his head and contemplated his axe.

"We tried to work from within the circle of our people, but the evil of men runs deeper then we could sound out. There is no running from it."

Nathaniel felt at home then, with his father's wise words flowing over him like water.

"Yes, on another day, it may be these British who take up arms against us," he said, looking around for a new path they could walk together.

His eyes then held theirs for the briefest of moments.

"But I don't mind trying to put it all behind us."

Red Blizzard

Ron Fortier

The snow had been falling since sunrise and the world appeared white and gray. Or so Hawkeye believed as he trudged through the calf-high drifts that blanketed the deep woods. The deer tracks he'd come upon were quickly being filled in by the thick, falling flakes and would soon be gone from sight. Thus it was all the more urgent for him to find the animal and bring it down. His stomach was empty having subsisted on dried hard jerky and corn biscuits for the past two days.

He hoped Chingachgook and Uncas were having better luck.

A gust of wind slid over the snow throwing up sheets that pelted him in the face, leaving him wet and cold despite his heavy leather coat and beaver cap.

Snap.

The barely audible sound of the breaking twig came from his front to the left. The deer tracks veered off towards the right. Hawkeye, born Nathaniel Poe, hefted his long Kentucky rifle in both his mitten covered hands and continued moving forward, his senses alert to the attack about to be sprung on him.

Suddenly the Mohawk brave stepped from behind a massive elm swinging a tomahawk over his head while screaming his lungs raw. He was caught off guard when Hawkeye charged into him, rather than stand frozen in surprise, the reaction he had been expecting. Instead the colonial woodsman brought up his rifle to block the tomahawk, stopping it in mid-decent and then, with a swiveling pivot of his hips, he turned sideways and shoved the stock of his weapon into the painted screaming face.

The butt broke the warrior's nose, sending bone shards into his brain, killing him on his feet. As the bloodied warrior fell another cry pierced the chilled air and Hawkeye dropped to one knee a second before another tomahawk whipped over his head, tearing off his thick fur hat. He pulled his huge, deadly hunting knife from the leather sash about his middle and with one fluid motion drove its point back into the groin of his second attacker, now off balance and falling over his right shoulder. He felt it tear through clothing and penetrate the man's belly. He twisted it hard and the brave cried again; this time in agony.

Why do they always yell? He thought, his mind racing like a jack-rabbit filing data and questions simultaneously as the attack materialized around him. *If stealth were the objective, then why purposely announce yourself to the enemy?*

Ignorant of how many braves had fallen upon him, Hawkeye dove forward under the collapsing body of the Mohawk he'd gutted, using it as a shield. His knife was caught in the man's gut and he let it go. A shot rang out just as he landed in the wet snow and he felt the body on his back jerk with the impact. With a mighty heave, he rose up, threw it off and aimed his rifle. Two leather clad figures were leaping at him. His finger, exposed through the slit in his mitten, pulled the trigger, the weapon bucked and his shot slammed into the nearest warrior throwing him backward into the air, a hole in his chest.

The fourth Mohawk kicked the rifle from his grasp at the same bringing his own rifle barrel down so that it was only inches from Hawkeye's face. Frantically the frontiersman reached up with both hands to grab the weapon just as the hammer dropped and pushed it to the side. The crack of the gun powder deafened him as the lead musket ball plowed into the snow inches from his left cheek.

Maintaining his grip on his foe's rifle, Hawkeye yanked it out of the Mohawk's hands and tossed it away. Retaliating quickly, the Indian, a tall, heavyset man, pulled his own rock-club from his belt and fell on him while raising his arm for a deadly swing.

Hawkeye caught the Mohawk's forearm with his hands and managed to stop the sharp chiseled stone from completing its arc into his face. His eyes glared up at the rage in his attacker's face; the brave was gritting his teeth in a snarl, so great was his desire to kill the white man. The top half of the warrior's face has been painted black and appeared demonic caught up in his bloodlust.

Desperately Hawkeye brought up his right leg, smashing his knee into the red man's back thus pushing him over his head. But at the same time he kept his grasp on the fellow's arm and was pulled along with him. As he began to roll atop the big Indian the earth beneath them suddenly collapsed as the wet snow cover let go like a sheered lip hanging over a steep slope.

Without warning both combatants, locked in their fierce death-grip, were sent tumbling over each other, their bodies falling faster and faster down the hillside dislodging other tightly packed fields of heavy white powder. Both of them were carried along in the center of a mini avalanche being hurled like so much flotsam down the side of the ravine, over brush and rock barely covered over, sliding past massive timbers to either side.

With the increased speed, Hawkeye and the Mohawk had forgotten all thought of their contest, each man solely focused on surviving their speedy fall. Then, just as they were nearing the base of the slope, they plowed into a giant pine tree, the impact ending their free flying tumble instantly. Each gave out with a loud groan as they made contact with the unyielding tower of wood.

They lay motionless on the ground, half buried in snow as the remainder of the cold wave passed them by. Slowly Hawkeye lifted up his head. The man beneath him was motionless, his neck twisted at a cruel angle indicating it had snapped upon hitting the pine, killing him instantly.

Gulping air, Hawkeye pushed away the snow and sat up, his back against the rough bark of the tree. As he tried to focus through his blurred vision, he gradually made out three other braves racing down the hill via the cleared path he and the dead Indian had inadvertently plowed during their rolling descent. Stars began to swim in his vision and he shook his head; pain flashed through his head and he winced. The closer the warriors came the more distinct they became until there was no doubt they were also Mohawks. Mohawks bent on revenging their fallen brothers.

Hawkeye's gun and knife were gone.

His body ached and his head was dizzy.

So this is how I am to die, he thought just before he lost consciousness.

Somewhere in the distance he heard more blood-curdling screaming.

"Will he live?'

"I believe so. Your white brother's head is hard like a rock."

The voices were familiar yet seemed to be coming from a far distance.

Hawkeye began to climb from the deep well of unconsciousness being pulled awake by those voices.

"He's coming around," the softer, older voice announced.

Hawkeye opened his eyes slowly and the wizened face before him solidified, its craggy, worn features split by the caring smile he treasured. Chingachgook, war chief of the Mohicans, had a stately look about him, with a granite-like face highlighted by a straight nose, high cheekbones and thick, gray eyebrows that matched his long hair; parted down the middle and tied into braids that framed his head.

He was the only father Hawkeye had ever known.

"Am I dead?" the scout asked starting to reach for his forehead. Gently his native stepfather pushed his hand back down.

"Not yet, my son, but you do have a goose-egg lump on your head. It will go away when the swelling goes down, if you leave it alone."

"A nice souvenir from the four Mohawks you danced with," the second voice said.

Standing behind Chingachgook was his handsome son, Uncas. With long flowing black hair and clean, honest features, the young man was a younger version of his father. He wore a mischievous smile while addressing his older, white stepbrother. "It was very selfish of you to leave us only three to deal with."

As his full senses returned, Hawkeye saw that he was propped up against another tree under which his father and brother had built a lean-to with gathered leaves woven together to make a canopy. Beyond them he could see a heavy snow continuing to fall and the dark twilight of dusk. A small campfire with a crackling flame was set near the edge of the shelter to allow the rising smoke to be sucked away by the outside wind.

"Water, please." Hawkeye's throat was parched. Uncas slipped a pouch off his shoulder and passed it to his father who in turn held it up for his white son to drink from. It was cold and delicious as it splashed into his mouth.

"How long have I been out?" he asked, wiping his lips with the back of his sleeve.

"Most of the day, my son," the elder Mohican answered. "Uncas and I were just about to take down a buck when we your heard your rifle speak. We raced over the hill just in time to see the remaining Mohawk dogs about to kill you. We shot two and the third fled rather than meet his end at our hands."

"You should have seen him run," Uncas chuckled, remembering the scene. "I would love to hear his lies when he returns to his people and tries to explain how eight warriors were routed by three."

A dark, fearsome look came over Chingachgook's face and he turned his head to spit on the ground. "They are a cursed, cowardly people who will one day be wiped away from these woods, when the Great Spirits mete out their justice."

Uncas exchanged a knowing glance with Hawkeye over their father's shoulder, regretting his comments immediately. Since the time of the Beaver Wars, decades earlier, the hated Mohawks had been the one tribe most responsible for the annihilation of the Mohican people of which only Chingachgook and Uncas remained. The tired war-chief's hatred of them was branded at the core of his very soul.

A whiff of something tasty assailed Hawkeye's nose and he blinked, sitting up a bit straighter. "What's that smell?"

"The turkey!" Uncas dashed to the fire and carefully reached down for the browned body of a roasting fowl. Not having had a clear view of the campfire, Hawkeye had failed to see the wooden spit on which the small, succulent wild bird was cooking.

"It is not deer or pheasant," Chingachgook shrugged, "but Uncas found several of these onerous, feathered beasts on the other side of the hill and brought one down with his hatchet. We won't go hungry this night."

As the young brave began cutting off chunks of hot turkey meat, Hawkeye observed a pile of rifles and hand weapons, some adorned with bird feathers, stacked to the right inside the lean-to.

"The spoils of war?" he said, indicating the stacked tools of combat.

"Yes," the elderly Mohican confirmed, turning to sit cross-legged next to Hawkeye. "They will make excellent gifts to our brothers, the Delaware, when we reach their village. It is less than a half day's walk from here, over the next hill."

Hawkeye took the next chunk of turkey from Uncas and began to bite into it. Forest turkeys had a hardy, nut-like taste most Indians did not care for but for the moment, safe and content with his family, the young frontiersman thought it the best meat he'd ever tasted.

The wailing song of the winter wind roused Hawkeye from his sleep in the middle of the night. He looked up, his eyes focusing on the shapes around him in the lean-to as provided by the light of the stars. The snow had let up and the heavens were a black field of tiny sparkling jewels men called stars.

To his right, by the cache of Mohawk weapons, stretched Uncas, on his side, snoring lightly.

Hawkeye raised up on his right elbow and beheld Chingachgook's silhouette as the Mohican sat looking out into the dark woods, his hands resting on the battle axe laid across his thighs.

"Father, do you converse with the dead?" Hawkeye whispered so as not to awaken Uncas.

"Yes," replied the wizened sachem. "When the world is quiet, a man can hear them speaking to his heart. It is a good thing to seek the council of those who have walked these paths before us."

"And what do they tell you?"

"That there will be more bloodshed in the days to come as the white man's greed spreads across these lands."

Hawkeye sat up, stretching his back muscles. "But why? Isn't there enough land and beaver for all?"

"So we believe, my son. But this greed, this longing to own what is given to us freely by the Great Spirit Mother is a sickness, Hawkeye. One our people are helpless to deal with."

"And the Mohawks, what is their part in all this?"

"They have allied themselves with the French," Chingachgook reasoned. "It is my thought they have been sent to threaten those people who might favor the British. To scare them with their tomahawks and long rifles."

"You think they plan to attack the village of the Delawares?"

"Yes. But we will warn them, Hawkeye. And if need be, we will fight with them."

Hawkeye let those words sink into his thoughts carefully examining all their implications.

From far off he heard soft growls and then tearing noises. He looked to Chingachgook.

"Our brothers, the wolves of the forest, have discovered the dead Mohawks," the wise Mohican said. "They are enjoying their feast."

The bright morning sky was a robin egg's blue by the time Chingachgook and his sons left their impromptu campsite and began trudging eastward over the steep foothills. The snow had ceased sometime in the night and left another thick layer well over seven inches deep across dense woodland terrain. Every step was an effort testing their physical strength and endurance.

It didn't help that each also carried crudely made sling-sacks over their shoulders filled with the fallen Mohawks rifles and hand weapons. Uncas had fashioned the pouches from the pants he'd removed from the dead men.

"I trust our Delaware brothers will appreciate these gifts," Hawkeye said wryly as he maneuvered around a boulder and stopped to catch his breath.

"My brother complains like an old woman," Uncas laughed, moving past Hawkeye and slapping him on the arm. "Is the climb too much for you, Hawkeye?"

"You disrespectful pup," the frontiersman retorted. "Let's see which one of us reaches the top of the rise first."

With that, Hawkeye propelled himself up the slope with an extra surge of determination, making his sore legs move faster to come up alongside the younger man. Seeing him catching up, Uncas leaned forward and joined the contest with gusto.

Below them Chingachgook chuckled and nodded his head in amusement. To the empty woods he said, "Ah, to have such energy to waste." He continued after his sons in the same slow and deliberate pace. Later, when he reached the clearing at the top of the hill, he found both Hawkeye and Uncas lying on the ground, both breathing heavily.

"Who is the victor?"

Hawkeye, grinning foolishly, pointed at Uncas who in turn sat up and pointed to Hawkeye. At this the brothers started laughing.

"I have raised a pair of fools," Chingachgook admitted, only to have his sons laugh all the harder.

Standing atop the crest of the hill, he had a clear view of a wide lake covered with ice and snow that sat between two majestic mountains. The Delaware village was five miles away on the opposite shore; a relatively short distance in a canoe. Whereas the winter was still young, the Mohican chief was leery of attempting to cross it on foot, not convinced the ice layer had hardened enough to support their weight. Their only course of action was to skirt the lake's southern edge and reach the village from that direction.

Admonishing his sons to quit their silliness, he started down the hill carefully heading for the bottom and the lake's edge.

They were half way to the base when a gunshot rang out and a chuck of elm bark exploded just over Uncas's head, peppering his cheek with tiny wooden shrapnel. It was followed by several other shots that zipped around them hitting trees and ground.

Attacking at them from behind were a dozen Mohawk warriors, all screaming. Most were brandishing tomahawks and war-clubs while others carried rifles.

"To the lake!" Chingachgook commanded as he crouched and began racing through the trees, Hawkeye and Uncas on his heels.

"It seems we've found the rest of the war party," Hawkeye yelled as more lead balls flew over their heads.

"Why do we not stand and fight?" Uncas blurted as he leaped high in the air over a clump of rocks.

"Because there are too many," his father explained, his sharp eyes darting back and forth amongst the trees as they recklessly descended. He had spotted other figures moving at them from both sides in a carefully planned pincer movement.

"We're trapped!" Uncas stated the obvious, seeing what his father had already spotted. "There must be at least fifty or more."

And just like that Chingachgook knew his earlier plan to circumvent the semi-frozen waters was no longer viable. The Mohawks had decided their fate leaving them only one option if they were to have any chance of survival; they were going to have to cross the lake and hope they could outrace their enemies.

As they came to an abrupt halt at the foot of the hill, they were only a few feet from the snow covered lake. Chingachgook slipped off the weapons pouch from his back and told his sons to do the same. "The ice will be thin; we must shed as much weight a possible."

Then he pulled his long, curved battle-axe from his shoulder and began to tap the slender tip through the snow crust to test the ice below.

Each time the tip broke through. Here the ice was paper thin and would not hold them.

Meanwhile, having divested themselves of their extra burdens, Hawkeye and Uncas had each grabbed a primed rifle from the cache they were abandoning and, hiding behind trees, returned fire. Hawkeye's shot took out a brave charging down the hill while Uncas hit another coming from their right flank.

Understanding the urgency of their plight, Chingachgook looked to both his right and left across the lake's border knowing the ice closest to shore would be brittle. Then he gave a silent thanks to the Manitous when he a saw a giant oak that had grown perilously close to the lake's edge and had long ago toppled into its waters; an action caused by either erosion of the earth around its roots or a powerful storm wind. Regardless of what had brought down the might timber, its body now stretched almost twenty yards into the lake and the Mohican prayed it had become a natural bridge to their salvation.

"Come," he called out, starting along the slim banking, doing his best to stay down and use the trees as cover. "This way, hurry!"

Uncas dodged around a small clump of bushes and followed carrying only his own weapons. Hawkeye fired one more rifle, this time dropping a warrior moving towards their goal, the fallen tree. He tossed aside the useless weapon, picked up his own Kentucky long rifle and another two and began chasing after his companions.

A half-dozen gunshots crashed into the tree-line while several spears and tomahawks also took flight after the three running men; all missed their mark.

Reaching the fallen oak, Chingachgook leaped atop it and began racing over its rotting bark weaving his way around the leafless branches that stood out like a broken picket fence. Uncas came hurrying behind him and half way across the giant tree slipped on the slick bark, one leg shooting out from beneath him. He frantically grabbed one of the thick branches and caught himself. Hawkeye rushed up behind him and, extending one of his rifle barrels, allowed Uncas to take hold and pull himself upright.

By now Chingachgook had come to the end of the tree and was once again using his war-club to test the solidity of the ice. He was rewarded with a loud, smacking noise as its tip pushed down through the snow blanket. He did this two more times and again hit solid ice that would not shatter. His heart leapt joyfully. They still had a chance.

Lead shots hit the crude tree wharf all around them and Chingachgook lost all hesitancy as he stepped out onto the frozen lake and began walking rapidly; the ice was slippery under his leather stocking and to run would be folly. Still he was moving at good clip.

Uncas came to the end of the fallen oak, saw his father's fearlessness and started to pursue. Hawkeye turned one last time, fired one of his extra rifles to keep the Mohawks at bay and then tossed it away. Then he was on the ice cautiously chasing after his family.

Chingachgook could feel cracks spidering under his feet and turning his head told his sons to move away and maintain a safe distance from each other as to not put their combined weights together.

Using his teeth, Hawkeye pulled off the mitten of his right hand and stuffed it into his coat as he set about moving himself between his Indian father and brother.

"Load your rifles and throw them to me," he called out. "I'll see about discouraging our friends." He had a smile on his handsome face that both Chingachgook and Uncas were all too familiar with. Hawkeye was the finest marksman on the frontier and in his hands the Kentucky long rifle was a death-spitting tool that never missed.

That said, the trio continued moving towards the center of the lake with the elder Mohican on Hawkeye's right and his stepbrother on his left. Both men had also removed their mittens and were expertly shoving black powder down the barrels of their rifles while maintaining their pace. Seeing their progress, Nathaniel stopped and slowly turned to look back at the shoreline. They had covered well over a hundred yards but the Mohawks had also come onto the ice having traced their own path over the toppled tree. They were clumped together and Hawkeye counted nearly two dozen of the painted braves.

One in particular stood by the exposed gnarled roots of the massive tree shouting encouragement to the others while waving his own tomahawk over his head and then pointing it at the fleeing trio; he was bald with a single braided pony-tail and the bottom half of his face had been painted cherry red while the top half, from his nose upward, was a frightening bone white. Hawkeye rightly assumed he was the war chief of the raiders.

Fueled by their leaders' loud ravings, the braves swarmed over the lake like red ants marching across spilled flour. They were hollering maddeningly as they charged onward. Several lost their footing and went down causing those behind them to trip over them and Hawkeye chuckled. Still, the more astute were shuffling their footsteps and coming for them with a determined bloodlust.

With an easy, fluid motion he brought the lightweight rifle to his shoulder and tilted his head to look over the flintlock percussion cap and lined up his front sight on the Mohawk in the lead. For a second he lifted his gaze to the treetops, felt a cold breeze on his left cheek and adjusted his aim to compensate for the wind. Taking an easy breath, he pulled the Maplewood stock into his shoulder at the same time squeezing the trigger. The cap ignited, the black powder exploded in a puff of foul smelling smoke and a second later the Mohawk soldier was knocked off his feet and fell back into the men behind him; dead.

Hawkeye spun around and continued following after Uncas and Chingachgook who had gained a good lead on him, which was what he wanted. His stepfather glanced back and nodded acknowledging his white son's bulls-eye as a nonchalant matter of fact. The Mohican had taught the orphaned Nathaniel Poe how to shoot and it was ever a thing of pride that the lad had become a veritable legend in the Colonies. He was known by several names throughout the woodland empire from Hawkeye, which Chingachgook and Uncas called him, to Deerslayer by friendly colonials, to *La*

Longue Carabine by the hated French up in the Canadas and their Indian allies.

Having traversed another twenty yards, Hawkeye called out to his stepfather.

"Now."

Chingachgook turned and tossed Hawkeye his primed rifle and in return Hawkeye threw him his empty one. Immediately, while still moving, the Mohican began to reload it while the sharpshooter once again stopped and prepared to bring down another Mohawk.

They had gained much distance between themselves and their foes. Hawkeye estimated they were close to two hundred yards apart. For an ordinary man it would be almost impossible to hit a target at that distance—but not for him.

"Shoot for those coming up on the sides," Chingachgook yelled. "Forget those in the front."

Hawkeye glanced back at his fleeing mentor with a puzzled expression. He didn't understand the older man's reasoning. Still he respected his stepfather and had seen his common sense wisdom displayed on hundreds of occasions. He wasn't about to argue the man's directive now when their lives depended on every move they made.

Hawkeye turned the barrel of his rifle away from those Mohawks leading the group and as advised set his sights on those straggling to the right of the oncoming party. A sigh, a squeeze of the trigger and another brave was knocked over.

Amazed at the lethal accuracy of his shot, the other Mohawks began to move closer together in a more compact body, each fearfully respecting the white man's prowess with the long rifle.

And in that movement, Hawkeye immediately understood Chingachgook's cunning. He laughed and once again started racing after his adopted kin.

Twenty more yards and this time Hawkeye called out to Uncas. Again an exchange of rifles was achieved with easy tosses between the two men. Uncas started reloading his empty weapon before Hawkeye had started to pick out his next target. By now all of them, hunters and hunted, were well across the lake far from the security of the shore.

The sun had come around Hawkeye's left shoulder and the snow blanket reflected its brilliance so that he had to squint to make out the Mohawks. Shooting through the blinding glare would be difficult but not impossible. This time he opted to aim for someone at the left of the oncoming war party even though the warriors in the lead were quickly narrowing the gap between them.

Hawkeye fired and was satisfied his shot was true but he took no personal satisfaction in his death-dealing marksmanship. Life in the wilderness was hard and there was no room for the weakness of mercy; kill or be killed was the Indian way. One he had been raised to accept without question.

These moral thoughts were passing through his mind when suddenly there was a loud, massive noise as if the world had cracked opened. The ice beneath his feet seemed to heave slightly and then he beheld a sight he would never forget all the days of his life.

Huge shards of crystal clear ice suddenly exploded upwards all around the front cluster of Mohawks and then they disappeared into the freezing waters. It happened so fast, not a single brave had time to cry out.

One second they were there and the next they were gone!

Chingachgook and Uncas, like Hawkeye, had ceased their flight and all three stood in transfixed awe watching the tragedy that had befallen their foes. Though many had gone under the exposed waters never to reappear, several of the warriors nearer the break's edges were desperately trying to pull themselves out of the frigid lake. The Mohicans and Hawkeye watched in silence as the struggling Mohawks tried vainly to save themselves.

More slipped from view, while others managed to heave themselves onto the fragile ice for a momentary respite only to have it shatter beneath them and once more plunge them into a watery doom. Those Mohawks beyond the reach of the rapidly expanding hole hurried back away to maintain their footing on safer ice. A few of the braver Indians stretched out on the cold surface extending their rifles or spears to those thrashing about in the water, doing their best to pull them to safety.

Caught up in viewing the drama, Hawkeye was shaken from his reverie when a voice cried out his name.

"*La Longue Carabine*!" He looked at the Mohawks and saw their leader, the one with the red and white war paint, standing off to the side behind the others, waving his tomahawk in the air to get his attention. "Do you hear me, *La Longue Carabine*?"

"I hear you," Hawkeye cupped his mitten-free hand next to his mouth and yelled. "How do you know me?"

The warrior stopped waving his weapon. "Only one man can shoot the long rifle with such skills." Then he thumped his chest with his tomahawk. "I am Koruk, war chief of the Mohawks."

"I see you, Koruk," Hawkeye called back.

Koruk nodded and then pointed his tomahawk at the scout. "I am going to kill the mighty *La Longue Carabine* and then I will cut out his eyes and carry them in my medicine bag as strong magic."

"Many others have tried," Hawkeye retorted. "They have all gone to join their people across the Great River. When next we meet, you will join them."

Koruk began waving his tomahawk over his head and screaming obscenities. Hawkeye turned his back on him and went to join Chingachgook and Uncas who had witnessed the exchange. The three kept their distance from each other, allowing Hawkeye to take the center spot between them.

"You have made a new enemy, my white son," Chingachgook observed dryly.

"It would appear so, father."

"Ha, ha, ha," Uncas chuckled as they began moving forward in unison. "It's your charming personality."

A black crow cawed overhead in the stark blue skies and the three men continued on their way.

It was mid-afternoon by the time the three travelers arrived at the eastern side of the frozen lake where the camp of the Delaware was located. Ominous gray clouds, propelled by a cold northwest wind, had overrun the sun and blotted it out completely. Chingachgook knew more snow was coming behind the fast moving front and he was glad their journey over the ice-lake had come to an end.

The Delaware village was huge, consisting of ten longhouses. Tribes of the Iroquois League were known as the Haudenosanee which translated to People of the Longhouses. These impressive structures were built between eighty and a hundred feet long and eighteen to twenty feet wide and each one housed up to twenty or more families, most of whom were matrilinearly related; it being the woman's ancestry that determined leadership. Poles were set in the ground and braced by horizontal poles along the walls, strips of bark were woven horizontally through lines of these poles to form weatherproofing walls with the doors on both ends covered with animal hide to maintain warmth. The roofs were constructed by bending a series of poles, resulting in an arc shape and then covered by leaves and grass. Holes were left in the roof at specific intervals to allow the smoke from interior cooking fires to escape.

Hawkeye could see dozens of such smoke columns rising up over the village.

A palisade of cut logs eighteen feet in height surrounded the Delaware community on three sides with the fourth facing a wide open beach area where several dozen canoes were pegged to the ground; between them a wooden wharf jutted out into the lake. It was for this structure the three men directed their footsteps.

Gathered on the beach end was a large contingent of Delawares, mostly armed men with a few brave females in the crowd and several curious youngsters in the rear trying to worm their way forward to see who was coming.

Chingachgook was not surprised by the welcoming committee as he knew the gunshots fired during their flight from the Mohawks had easily echoed across the lake and alerted the villagers. Of course the last thing any of them had expected to see an hour later was three weary figures approaching their dock across the frozen waters.

As the Mohican stepped onto the wharf, he held up his empty right hand; a gesture to indicate their peaceful intentions. Chingachgook recognized the white haired sachem coming forward to greet them followed by several fit, young braves; he was named Netatwees and like Chingachgook had been raised as a youth in the Turtle Clan.

The two men met in middle of the ice-encased platform and clasped forearms together in friendship.

"My eyes are happy to set upon my Mohican cousin, Chingachgook," the older man smiled, his taut, bronzed features still ruggedly handsome with his advanced years though his brown eyes were remarkably clear.

"As are mine to behold the sachem of the Delawares. This is a good day for us, cousin."

"But why do Chingachgook and his sons travel across the frozen waters in such a manner?"

"We were chased by a large band of Mohawk raiders and had no choice but to risk the ice." Chingachgook swept his arm back towards the lake. "The Great Spirit guided our feet safely across."

"And what of the Mohawk dogs?" asked the tall youth standing to Netatwees' left. He was a massive fellow with a powerful physique and granite-like features and wore three eagle feathers in his long black hair.

"We killed some with our rifles and the lake claimed many others," Chingachgook addressed his reply to the tall brave. "But the rest, thirty or so, are still back there and pose a threat to your village."

"This is Tamenend, my son," the chief said, introducing the big Indian lad.

"It is good to meet the son of my cousin," the Mohican politely responded and then indicated his own sons. "These are my sons, Uncas and his white brother, Hawkeye."

"Come," Netatwees said, "let us continue this reunion in the warmth of our longhouse where we will have food to eat and you can rest."

"Your kindness is most welcome," Chingachgook nodded and he and his sons followed their hosts over the beach and into the nearest longhouse.

Hawkeye detested the confines of the huge longhouse because, despite its spaciousness, the interior was still dark and affected the outdoorsman's innate claustrophobia. There had to be over a hundred people crammed together in Netatwees' longhouse and the smells of so many bodies, skinned hides, cooking pots etc. all assaulted his sensitive nose with their foulness. As one who preferred the openness of the great wilderness where the stars made a wondrous roof for the entire world, the scout's internal fortitude was tested. He had all he could do to go along with Chingachgook and Uncas in joining their host around a cooking fire located at the center of the long structure.

Whereas the building had no windows, common among colonial log cabins, the only light emanated from the crackling fires and they were weak; unable to define the milling men, women and children constantly moving to and fro around them.

I will never live in such a place, Hawkeye promised himself as he sat down on the hard earth around the center blaze with his family. Adjusting his legs, one over the other, he felt a slight overhead breeze and looked up to see the smoke escaping through the hole directly above them. He was grateful for even this small gust of cool air.

Once all were seated, several women, one the sachem's wife, began dolling out wooden bowls filled with a tasty venison stew. Hawkeye scooped up a gob with his fingers and shoveled it into his mouth. It tasted wonderful and he thanked their host for such a delicious meal. Several of the younger women infatuated by his and Uncas' good looks blushed at his compliment and then, satisfied their guest had been well served, disappeared once more in the gloom beyond he fire's glow.

When all had eaten and set down their empty bowls, the two chiefs began to converse, each relating all that had transpired since their last meeting. It was clear to Chingachgook that his elderly cousin was troubled by something and he politely inquired as to what the matter was.

"Your instincts are as sharp and keen as ever, Chingachgook," Netatwees smiled through sad eyes. "Early this morning it was discovered that two of our young people had run off during the middle of the night."

Chingachgook merely nodded, knowing the sachem would tell the tale in his own fashion, but he did see Tamenend stiffen his back when his father began to speak of the incident.

"One was Sagawa, student of Totten, leader of our False Face Society."

At the mention of the tribe's primary medicine man, he suddenly materialized behind the sitting sachem, arms folded across his chest. He was of average height with gray hair tied in a ponytail and a thin, angular face marked by piercing black eyes. He was attired in buckskin clothing beautifully decorated with hundreds of colored beads.

"Sagawa is my most talented student," the shaman explained. "Though often a slave to his heart."

"He is a thief and nothing more!" Tamenend suddenly blurted out, rising to his feet and pointing at Totten. "He has stolen my bride-to-be and must be caught and punished for this black deed."

Both Hawkeye and Uncas looked at each other, Nathaniel giving his brother a quick blink of the eye. Things were starting to get interesting, each thought simultaneously.

Old Netatwees looked up at his son and sighed heavily before addressing his guest once more. "Tamenend is to marry the maid, Kateri. This was agreed upon by her parents and he paid them with many fine beaver furs. The entire village was eager to celebrate their union.

"Then this morning it was learned both Sagawa and Kateri had fled." The sachem looked up at his angry son choosing his words carefully. "Some have said Kateri's heart already belongs to Sagawa and so they …"

"Lies!" Tamenend cried out once again, accusing Totten with a pointing finger. "Sagawa used black magic to sway Kateri and spirit her away."

"That remains to be proven," Totten rebutted, his voice remaining steady and calm. "Until they are found and returned, the truth will remain hidden."

"And that is our dilemma," Netatwees continued. "We were about to send out a searching party to find them when we heard the echoes of your encounter with the Mohawks. Now, upon hearing of their presence in these woods, I cannot send out our braves on a foolish hunt and leave our village undefended should the surviving Mohawks launch an attack."

"Then I will go alone," declared Tamenend, pounding his burly chest with his fist. "I require no assistance in bringing back a frail seer and a squaw."

"And what of the coming storm, my son?" Netatwees asked, looking back at his medicine man. "Totten has said the mother of all storms is soon to be upon us."

"I have survived storms before," the youth replied.

"Not like this one," the leader of the False Face Society warned, spreading out his hands in a widening gesture. "The signs portent a savage fury of cold and snow will fall upon the very mountains that shield us. If you are caught unprepared, you will surely die."

A heavy silence descended on the gathering as Totten's portent weighed heavily on all who had heard it.

Finally Netatwees, his face lined with worry, looked to Chingachgook. "What I am to do, old friend?"

"Your duty is clear, cousin," Chingachgook explained. "Even if this bad storm falls upon the mountains, your warriors must not leave your palisades as the Mohawk could use the storm to conceal their attack.

"My sons and I will go after the runaways for you. You forget, cousin; I was raised in these woods. I know every cave and natural shelter in these mountains. If Sagawa and Kateri are to be found, it is a task we are well suited for."

"Thank you, Chingachgook, I accept your offer."

"But I will go with them," the obnoxious Tamenend interrupted. "It is my right."

Netatwees started to admonish his son for his rudeness only to have Chingachgook put a hand on his arm to stop him. "Tamenend is welcome and may prove of much assistance in our hunt."

"Then it is settled," the sachem of the Delawares confirmed. "We will provide you with both provisions and powder for our rifles and you can depart at first light. May the Manitous of our people guide your search."

At that everyone seemed relieved that the matter had been resolved. For his part, Hawkeye looked at Tamenend's smug features and once again exchanged a glance with Uncas. This was one foretold of future troubles ahead. Uncas nodded in agreement.

Hawkeye could hear the wind sweeping over the lake while the night around him seemed devoid of life. His feet moved but didn't touch the ground and he knew he was dreaming. He was going to the small dock and could see a man standing there facing the mountains beyond the lake.

Hawkeye knew it was Totten, the leader of the False Face Society.

"Why am I here?" he inquired.

Totten turned and Hawkeye was startled to see him wearing the long, garish wooden mask of his sect. It had wide round eyes and a long painted slit for a mouth.

"Tamenend is ruled by anger and jealously," the medicine man told him. "In this anger he will desire to kill Sagawa. You must not let this happen."

"Why do you not tell my father?" Hawkeye was confused.

"His mind is on saving all. He will not understand the importance of what he does."

Totten stepped closer and leaning forward brought his awful mask up to Hawkeye's face. "Sagawa will one day be a great medicine man. You must heed his words, Nathaniel Poe."

Hawkeye was surprised by the use of his Christian name.

An owl suddenly swooped down out of the sky and hooted, its claws reaching for his face.

The scout sat up with a gasp.

He was back in the longhouse with Chingachgook and Uncas peacefully asleep only a few feet away from him next to the dying fire. The images from his dream slowly began to fade as he lay back down in hopes of going back to sleep.

Still he heard Totten's warnings in his mind as he closed his eyes.

The next morning Hawkeye chose not to mention his dream encounter with the medicine man, afraid it would complicate their mission and just be another weight on Chingachgook's shoulders. Instead he helped his stepfather and Uncas pack the provisions Netatwees people provided them into sturdy deerskin packs and then with the brave, Tamenend, taking the lead, they departed the village of the Delawares and started their climb into the bordering mountains.

As the gates of the palisades were closing behind them, Hawkeye caught a glimpse of Totten standing behind the group that had come to see them off. The medicine man's face revealed no emotion, only a stoic acceptance of what would come of their quest. The scout wondered if that kind of emotional detachment was something to be admired or despised; crazy notions he quickly dispelled. Their only concern had to be finding the runaway couple before the oncoming storm made that task impossible.

For the rest of the morning they traveled upward on a narrow, winding path that cut into the side of the granite mountain until the terrain became devoid of most vegetation save an occasional thorny bush pushing out between massive boulders. The sky overhead was ominously dark as fast moving gray clouds totally hid the sun and the temperature began to drop the higher they climbed.

Eventually tiny drops of rain began to fall on them making the rocky path slick and they had to move cautiously. The rain quickly morphed into fat snowflakes and soon their ears were popping as they reached even higher elevations.

Although he had no fear of heights, Hawkeye was still leery as the footpath shrunk at several spots so that they were only inches from empty space to their right. The Delaware village and the lake were thousands of feet below them. Strong gusts of wind threatened to yank them off the small ledge and, walking single file, each man gritted his teeth while carefully continuing to move onward.

When they reached a flat plateau that extended eastward and was dotted with woods, Chingachgook called for a rest. The heavy snow continued to fall as the four huddled together under the thick bows of several evergreens and sat on the hard, wet ground to eat from their traveling kits.

"How much higher does this mountain go?" Uncas asked his father as he bit into a piece of deer jerky.

"There are several plateaus above this one where there are many caves," Chingachgook answered, pointing to the edge of the copse of trees where the side of mountain continued upward. "It has been many years since I was last here, but I believe this is where our quarry would seek shelter."

Tamenend took a sip of water from a boar-gut pouch and nodded. "You are correct." He pointed up towards the nearly invisible peaks above them. "Sagawa, like all our people, knows the location of those caves. I am sure that is where he has taken Kateri to wait until the storm passes."

"And then?" Hawkeye spoke up. "Where do you think he is going?"

"Beyond to the edge of the great waters and the land you whites call Virginia," Tamenend surmised, sharing his thoughts. "Many of our people trade with the settlements there. That is where Sagawa will go."

Hawkeye began to say something else when the echo of a rifle shot interrupted him. Instantly all for men were alert, each grabbing his weapons and surveying the surrounding woods with sharp eyes.

Chingachgook rose to one knee and motioned to Uncas with his fingers to go and seek out who had fired the shot. As his son gripped his rifle tightly and slid away in a crouch, the Mohican leader turned to Hawkeye and Tamenend and whispered, "Stay low and find shelter until Uncas returns."

Without any further directions, the three each found a suitable boulder or tree to hide behind within eyesight of each other. They made sure their rifles were primed and then waited in silence for what would happen next. Hawkeye wondered if by luck they had actually stumbled on the lad, Sagawa, thinking it may have been Totten's protégé who had fired the shot.

Five minutes later Uncas returned as quietly as he had departed and in a whisper told them their luck was anything but good. "It is our old friends, the Mohawks," he reported after the four had huddled together, staying down beneath clumps of rocks and bushes. "They were busy gutting a buck when I spied them." He pointed to the south and stated the remaining Mohawks were approximately twenty-five to thirty in numbers.

"They must have circled the lake and come up along another trail," Chingachgook deduced, directing his remarks to Tamenend. "They must still be intent on attacking your village."

"There is another threat here," Hawkeye whispered. "What happens if they stumble on any tracks left by Sagawa and the maid Kateri?"

A look of genuine concern crossed the tall Delaware's features. "Then it is all the more important we find them first."

"Agreed," Chingachgook said. "Come, we must find the trail to the next plateau before our enemies have finished their meal and pass this way."

With that the four began jogging through the trees once again continuing their journey up the cold, dangerous mountain trail. All around them the wind howled and the snow continued to spill from the dark skies.

The storm grew in intensity as the afternoon lengthened and the four heavily-clothed travelers wound their way up the side of the mountain, each doing his best to keep up with the man in front of him. With the gale reaching a blinding ferocity it became impossible to see beyond a few feet and Chingachgook sensed Tamenend's hesitancy the further along they climbed. The young brave was unsure of the path and the older Mohican worried he might carelessly lead them to walk straight off the edge of a precipice. Thus he had taken the lead, ordering Tamenend to swap places with him. Once in the lead, Chingachgook mentally ignored the howling wind and pressed forward with a powerful resolve while keeping his left hand out to maintain contact with the hard wall.

Several times shadowy figures darted across the path before them; appearing and disappearing from the swirling white world around them. Chingachgook thought he recognized a mountain goat and later a long-tailed red fox. Like them, the four footed dwellers of these ranges were desperate to seek shelter before the cold froze their limbs and stole the breath from their lungs. As a young brave, Chingachgook had once beheld the corpse of a helpless brave who had frozen to death, his face covered with blue ice and his limbs stiff as tree bark. He had no desire to cross over the Great River in such a gruesome manner.

Taking a step around several loose rocks, Chingachgook's nose smelled a fait burnt odor. Smoke? Brushing snow from his face with his thick mitten, he tried to peer through the curtain of snow while sniffing like an animal to catch the elusive scent. There it was again; he was smelling smoke. Then he made out a very faint pink glow through the blizzard and moved to it all the while hoping his three companions were still following him. He had no way of knowing, so loud was the tempest that assailed him and deafened his hearing.

The glow he had seen was becoming brighter turning to a yellow color. Then, as if materializing from a world of vague, mind numbing cold, he was suddenly stepping into the mouth of a cave which instantly appeared in sharp relief due to the small burning campfire before him. He moved around it quickly as his companions came stumbling in behind him until all four stood shivering, transfixed around the crackling flames feeding off a clump of thick bushes and twigs patted together and circled with heavy stones.

Slowly Hawkeye, frost covering his eyebrows, pushed back his coat's hood and shook his head, feeling the warmth of the fire kiss his face. The others did the same with both Uncas and Tamenend dropping to their knees, removing their mittens and putting their hands as near the flames as they could endure.

"Who goes there?" a voice called out from the cave's black interior.

They all looked up as a young Delaware brave stepped forward holding a hatchet in his hands menacingly. Clutching his free arm was a lovely Indian maid, her doe-like brown eyes wide with fear.

Hawkeye grinned at his stepfather. "It appears we have found our runaways."

The young Mohawk warrior named Machu marched through the snowstorm mentally cursing his war chief, Kurok, for leading them away from the warmth of their wigwams on this foolish raiding party. They had already lost half their numbers the previous day while attempting to chase the fleeing Mohicans and the white called *La Longue Carabine*.

Machu and his friends thought for sure Kurok would have given up this folly of a mission and returned to their own lands. But the painted war chief was obsessed with finding the white marksman and his companions more than ever and they compelled them to circumnavigate the lake and enter the mountains from the south.

At first the jaunt had been trouble-free and taking down the giant buck with the huge wrack of antlers had provided them with much-needed sustenance. At one point, Machu and the other young braves began to believe the Manitou might be actually favoring their raid.

Then the sky turned black and the sharp, stinging snows returned. Within minutes the Mohawks were lost in the blizzard, stumbling about the mountain plateau with no idea where they were headed.

Which was when Machu tripped over a tree root jutting out of the ground and landed face first in the snow. Angry, he started to pick himself up when he spotted something small and dark in the field of white before his face. He reached up and scooped it up, brining it closer to get a better look at what it was he had found almost buried by the falling flakes.

And then Machu was on his feet crying out to Kurok and the others who all came running to him. Surrounded by their anxious faces, he looked at his chief and handed him what he'd discovered.

It was a piece of deer jerky several inches long showing teeth marks at one end.

The implication of it still being fresh and on the ground here was not lost on the wily Kurok. "Where did you find this?" he demanded.

Machu went over by the tree whose roots had tripped him and pointed down. Kurok bent down and studied the spot. His keen eyes looked around the area and he could just barely make out footprints below the layers of newly fallen snow. Someone had been here only a short while ago, of that he was certain.

As he rose up slowly, his remaining braves waited in silence for whatever declaration he would make, but Kurok was surveying the plateau trying to guess where the makers of the footprints had gone. His black eyes fell on the mountain wall and his instincts told him whoever they were, they had taken the path upwards.

He raised up his tomahawk and gave out a war cry. "Come," he told his Mohawks. "We must hurry if we are to catch whoever made these tracks!"

Kurok began racing for the mountain trail. The thought of catching their enemies by surprise heated his blood and made him forget the blasting cold that ran with them.

Sagawa was much as Hawkeye had imagined in his mind; a tall, thin fellow with a sharp, angular face, his nose crooked from a long ago break. His eyes were small like a bird's but with the same intense stare seeming to take in everything all at once.

Whereas Kateri was beyond the white man's experiences as he had never beheld a maiden so beautiful before. She was almost as tall as Sagawa, with a deep, burnished skin, a V-shaped face with taut cheek bones, delicate full lips and two almond shaped brown eyes that were simply mesmerizing.

All this Hawkeye took in as the two fugitives emerged from the cave's interior, both clutching each other in mortal fear. Upon seeing Kateri, the scout could understand why Tamenend was so determined to reclaim her from his rival. As to what such a maid could see in an awkward, gangly man like Sagawa was beyond Hawkeye's comprehension. Chingachgook, when speaking of matters of the heart, often told him and Uncas that love was blind. Now he believed it.

"Tamenend!" Kateri blurted out upon recognizing her recent betrothed.

"Yes, it is I," the Delaware prince said, moving past the fire to confront the couple at the same time his left hand grabbed the knife from his leather belt.

Immediately Sagawa pushed Kateri back and moved to intercept the angry Tamenend.

To his credit, the medicine man's student demonstrated his own courage by shielding the girl without a thought to his own safety, though he did bring up his hatchet in a defensive stance.

Before the volatile Tamenend could reach the target of his rage, Chingachgook speedily intercepted him, coming to stand before the startled Sagawa, his arms pushing against Tamenend massive chest.

"Get out of the way, Mohican!" Tamenend's voice was filled with rage. "I will deal with this pathetic creature who would steal another man's woman!"

"No!" Chingachgook held his ground and both Hawkeye and Uncas took up positions to either side of Tamenend, making their intent perfectly clear. Move against Chingachgook and he would have to deal with all three of them.

Just then Kateri moved to Chingachgook's left and pointed her finger at her former suitor. "No one stole me! That is your lie, Tamenend, and well you know it to be so."

"But Kateri…."

"My heart has always belonged to Sagawa," the girl went on, refusing to let the big Indian dissuade her. "Everyone in our village knows this to be true but you, and that is only because you refuse to see the truth of it. Wishing it were not so will not aid your cause but only shame you further."

Having spoken her mind, Kateri backed up to once again stand by Sagawa, who wrapped his free arm around her shoulder, a defiant look on his face.

Slowly the tension in the cave began to dissipate with Tamenend's inability to respond to the maid's declaration. It was clear to everyone that she had merely stated the truth and now confronted with it head-on, the brave had no other recourse but to accept it no matter how painful it was to his pride. His knife hand lowered as did his head and hurriedly he turned his back on the others and returned to the campfire by the entrance.

Chingachgook released a long sigh of relief and smiled at Hawkeye and Uncas. Perhaps they just might complete this task without further problems.

Which was when the screaming Mohawk warrior came charging out of the storm into the cave, his tomahawk high over his head, his painted visage set in a blood-curdling scream.

Tamenend only had enough time to look up before the crazed Indian jumped boldly over the fire at him.

Instinctively Tamenend reached up with both hands and caught the arm coming down at him. With his mittened hands wrapped around it, he spun around putting his backside into the still forward moving Mohawk and, bending at the hips, flung the warrior over his shoulder and onto his back to land only inches from the startled Mohican and his sons.

Before the man could get up, Uncas drove the butt of his rifle into his face and silenced him forever. Kateri, hand over her mouth, stifled a scream.

Another Mohawk appeared at the entrance of the cave charging forward like his fallen brother; but this one only went a few feet before Hawkeye's lead ball smacked into his breast and knocked him back into the swirling blizzard outside.

Tamenend had scrambled to his feet and was arming himself, his long-bladed knife in his left and his wicked tomahawk in his right, all the time keeping his eyes on the opening beyond the campfire. His companions stood with him. Hawkeye quickly pulled a powder pouch from his coat and hastily reloaded his long rifle.

All five men and the Indian maid watched the cave opening, expectantly awaiting the next assault.

"*La Longue Carabine*," a voice barely heard about the storm winds called out to them and Hawkeye recognized it immediately. "It is I, Kurok, come to take your life as I promised."

"What are you waiting for?" the scout shouted back. "We have a warm fire waiting for you and your men. Come join us."

No one expected the crazed Mohawk to reply.

Chingachgook looked around the tight cave and shook his head. "We have to get out of this cave or surely we will die here."

"But there is another way out," Sagawa said. The others all turned to him and Kateri and he pointed back into the stygian darkness beyond. "We explored these passages earlier and there are several tunnels that come out on the eastern slope of the mountain."

Chingachgook slapped the young man on the arm and chuckled. "Then what are we doing still standing here? Lead the way, my young friend."

With Hawkeye and Tamenend watching the entrance, Uncas went to the fire and carefully pulled out a thick burning branch and handed it to Sagawa.

"Uncas and I will follow you," Hawkeye told his stepfather. Chingachgook merely nodded and then prodded the other to get moving. Sagawa held the burning brand outward and sure enough its flames illuminated a corner at the rear of the main tunnel. Soon he was moving around it followed by Kateri, Tamenend and Chingachgook.

Hawkeye and Uncas watched the glow of the torch on the back wall begin to diminish quickly until the others were far off and the impenetrable shadows once again hid the cave's exit.

"How long do we wait?" Uncas asked.

Hawkeye started to answer when another two Mohawks came rushing into the cave. Both the scout and his step-brother lifted their rifles in unison and fired simultaneously, creating a loud bang that rang off the stone walls.

The warrior on the right was hit in the shoulder and spun around, causing him to fall on his side into the campfire, while Hawkeye's bullet hit his man in the forehead and ripped out the back of his skull. The brave collapsed never to rise again.

The brave who had fallen amongst the flames started yelling as he frantically threw himself out of the fire and started beating at the sleeve of his right arm that was now ablaze. Uncas, again using his rifle butt like a hammer, slammed it into the back of the burning man's head, knocking him senseless.

"How about now?" Hawkeye suggested mischievously as he pulled a burning branch from the fire and held it up.

"After you, my brother."

Both men raced towards the hidden tunnel, Hawkeye using the flaming stick to light their way. Soon they too were gone deeper into the natural byways of the mountain leaving only four dead Mohawks in the cave behind them.

The mountain tunnel twisted and turned like a meandering forest brook and Chingachgook, the last in line after Sagawa, Kateri and Tamenend, kept glancing back over his shoulder in hopes of seeing his sons. He had heard the faint popping sounds of gunfire and could only hope Hawkeye and Uncas had triumphed in their continued battle with the tenacious Mohawks.

While they continued to hurry along the cramped rock-ways, Chingachgook introduced himself to the runaways and told them of how he and his sons had volunteered to find them for their sachem, Netatwees. After that all of them were quiet, each lost in their own thoughts for the next twenty minutes.

"There," Sagawa finally called out to the others. "We are coming to the end and I can see the night sky."

Chingachgook looked around Tamenend's broad back and could see the outlines of a gray circle ahead. With each step Sagawa's improvised torch defined the new portal in sharp relief.

Reaching it, all four stepped into the winter night and discovered it was a great deal more temperate than what they had endured on the western face of the mountain. Chingachgook looked up at the rising peak overhead and said a silent prayer of thanks. The storm that had been slamming into the western side of the lofty mountain was contained there and all they had to deal with on this leeward slope was the falling snow.

"Put out the torch," the Mohican ordered and Sagawa complied immediately, shoving its burning tip into the snow. "We need to let our eyes adjust to the night so that we don't go walking off a cliff."

"Then why did you have Sagawa put out our only light?" Kateri asked perplexed.

"Because," Tamenend explained. "If the Mohawks continue to pursue us, it will give away our location."

"Oh?" The girl was suddenly ashamed for having questioned Chingachgook but he showed no annoyance at her ignorance of such things.

As their eyes became used to the gray cast of the world around them, Chingachgook moved in front of the three youths and gave them further instructions.

"From this point, I will go first. We will proceed in single file with Sagawa behind me, then Kateri and Tamenend.

"Tamenend, listen carefully for any noise from behind as my sons should soon be catching up to us. I do not want them taking a different path than ours."

"I will do as you say, Chingachgook."

Gone was the big Indian's false bravado and recklessness. Apparently direct confrontation with Kateri and then the attack by the Mohawks had altered his attitude for the better.

"The trail appears to drop sharply," Chingachgook continued. "So we must be cautious and plant each footstep carefully."

Having nothing else to tell his charges, the Mohican warrior adjusted the sling of this war-axe on his back to a more comfortable position and then started down the mountain. Sagawa followed behind him while Kateri held on to her lover's back. Tamenend took one final glance over his shoulder at the cave opening and then followed the others.

As they descended further and further, a lonely night owl hooted reminding them they were not alone. All manner of beasts from badgers to coyotes lived in these mountains and did not always welcome two-legged intruders.

Suddenly Chingachgook came to an abrupt stop and Sagawa nearly walked into him.

"What is it?"

"We've come to the end of the path," Chingachgook said. "Be careful, we are standing on the lip of a giant crack in the earth."

Slowly the other three moved around the Mohican to stand in line with him and peer into the gloom ahead. Each was taken aback by the chasm that stretched before them, the opposite cliff barely visible on the other side.

Kateri grabbed Sagawa's hand and looked down and for a second was dizzy. All she could see was blackness and instinctively she knew the drop was lethal, perhaps extending to the base of the mountain thousands of feet below.

"What do we do now?" she gasped. "There's no way across."

Chingachgook heard the girl's words but continued to stare into the blackness ahead, his mind attempting to calculate the actual distance across the gap. One of the features he was aware, if only vaguely, was that the opposite cliff and ground was a few feet below their own. He could imagine the dawn of time when a cataclysmic quake had shaken these mountains and the spirits had cleaved the land in two, and the one half had settled beneath the other.

This was extremely important to their current situation. If they could jump the space then they would be falling downward onto the other ridge rather than trying a desperate leap where both sides were at the same level. It was the smallest of advantages but one they had to seize.

"You are wrong," he finally responded to Kateri's remark. "It is possible we can jump across."

"Are you serious?" Sagawa turned to the Mohican. "I can barely see the other ledge and it appears at least twenty feet away."

"That is what I calculate also," Chingachgook agreed.

"It is too far," Sagawa argued.

"Not if we get a good running start before we make our leap." He put his hand on Sagawa's right shoulder and gripped it confidentially. "If we don't try, then the Mohawks will soon find us and we will all die on this mountain. There is no other way, lad."

The young student of magic bit his lower lip, wanting to believe Chingachgook, but one nagging doubt remained. "Perhaps that is true of we men, but what of Kateri? She has never had to run or jump like this before. Her legs won't carry her that far."

"Which is why you and Tamenend will jump first," Chingachgook elaborated. "Once safely across, both of you will take up positions by the cliff's edge and should she fall short, one of you will catch her." Chingachgook pointed at the other ledge. "See, it is lower. If Kateri can get a good jump, she will be falling to you."

A heavy silence imposed itself on the four.

Sagawa still didn't like what the cunning Mohican was proposing. Kateri meant everything to him and should she fall to her death he would forever blame himself.

"Chingachgook is right," Kateri said ending the debate. "There is no other way…"

Gunshots sounded behind them and Chingachgook realized their time had run out. Whatever befell them, it had to be decided now.

"Tamenend," he directed. "You go first. Hurry!"

Having exited the tunnels minutes earlier, Hawkeye and Uncas, using their own burning branch, had found Sagawa's torch stuck in the snow. Uncas threw his own down on the ground and stamped it out with his leather stockings.

"Can you see them?" he asked Hawkeye. "Father and the others?"

The white scout faced the steep slope before them and squinted, doing his best to peer in to the night. "No, but I can see their footprints in the snow, my brother."

"Good, then let us follow."

Watching their steps, the two frontiersmen started down the mountain, the falling snow making each footstep a treacherous, unsure act.

They had only gone twenty yards when there was a loud clamoring of voices from behind them. Together they twisted around and looked up at the mouth of the cave from which they had just emerged. Another glowing light materialized from within the cave; this one held up by a Mohawk brave leading a half dozen warriors.

"Damn it," Hawkeye cursed. "I thought we'd left them behind."

"Then you were wrong," Uncas chuckled as he brought up his rifle. "Just don't make a habit out of it."

Uncas fired and the torch-wielding Mohawk cried out and tumbled to the ground. Before the others could react, a second round messenger of doom, this one from Hawkeye's long rifle, barked and a second Indian fell dead.

The Mohawks retreated back to the safety of the rock cave and then began returning fire with the rifles they possessed. Though they could not see where Hawkeye and Uncas were, Kurok, their leader, had seen the muzzle flashes and directed their fire.

Once again, holding their empty rifles before them, Chingachgook's sons began high-tailing down the trail.

Tamenend had retraced his steps away from the chasm to a distance of twenty yards in as straight a path as he could determine in the dark. All of them worried they might trip over a loose rock, hidden root or whatever but they had no other choice.

Chingachgook, Sagawa and Katcri watched as the tall, fearless Delaware folded into a crouch and gave the ground before him a final inspection. Then, with an ear splitting yell, Tamenend bolted forward into his run, his powerful legs pounding on the snow-packed rock and eating up yards.

Then the blackness of the fault loomed ahead of him and Chingachgook, unable to contain his own nerves, shouted out, "NOW! JUMP!"

Tamenend hurled himself into the air and flew across the emptiness that divided the two ledges. Cold air whipped past his face and he gritted his teeth and shapes suddenly appeared below him; boulders strewn across the rock surface upon which he was falling fast. He braced himself for the impact, his leather-clad feet hitting the unyielding granite floor only a few feet from the drop-off.

Then he was tumbling forward, bruised and battered but safe.

"Tamenend?"

"I made it," he called back to the Mohicans and the others. "Come, Sagawa. It is not that hard at all."

Bolstered by Tamenend's success, Sagawa let go of Kateri's hand and whispered. "Do not be afraid, we will be there to a catch you. I promise." Then he kissed her lightly on the cheek before jogging to the spot where Tamenend had started his sprint.

Like the big warrior, Sagawa took a crouched stance and then, taking a deep breath, took off at a full-out run, both his legs and arms pin-wheeling in unison. An icy fear gripped his heart as he reached the cliff but he pushed it aside and imagined himself a living spear. Into the air he went, his limbs still pumping as if he could walk across the very air.

As he started to fall, he saw the lip of the cliff and thought for a second he wouldn't reach it. Then his feet struck past it by mere inches. The jolt affected his balance and he began to fall backwards.

Tamenend's arms appeared, grabbed hold of his coat and pulled him away from the precipice to a secure footing. Sagawa sagged down and his fellow Delaware kept his grip firm, keeping him upright.

"Well done, medicine man," Tamenend complimented. "You have the courage of a true warrior."

Chingachgook and Kateri could hear the two conversing though their exact wording was indecipherable. The only thing that mattered to the lovely maiden was that her man had survived. Now it was her turn.

"Be brave," Chingachgook said as she started down the path to the starting place.

"I'll try," she promised.

As she found the mark, Chingachgook leaned over the cliff and yelled to Sagawa and Tamenend to be ready for her; that she was coming.

A thousand thoughts flooded Kateri's mind in that instant. Thoughts of her young life up to this moment, of all her trials and tribulations and how everything prior had all led to this one test of her courage. Then she realized what her mother had taught her from childhood was true: all of life was held in the hands of the Great Spirits. If they willed her to succeed, then she would. If not, then she would die trying and her people would know she had been brave.

Kateri began running, her heart pounding in her chest wildly. Manitou, she prayed. I come to you on the wings of my ancestors. Far off she could hear Chingachgook yelling for her to jump and then everything was a blur she would never remember, except in her dreams as an old woman of her people.

Tamenend and Sagawa had positioned themselves five feet apart, hoping to cover as much area as possible wherever the girl would come down. There just was no way to tell. They heard the Mohican's command to jump and then before their amazed eyes, Kateri, maid of the Delawares, was soaring through the air faster and higher than either had gone. She went past them like a gliding eagle and landed many feet behind them where she instantly passed out.

When Tamenend called out that Kateri had made it across, a broad happy smile covered Chingachgook's rugged face. There was something about Kateri that has reminded him of his own squaw, the true center of his heart, gone these many years. That Kateri had succeeded to make the leap confirmed his belief that she was another remarkable woman who had a very long future ahead of her.

But now he had to worry about his own future.

More gunshots echoed from the top of the slope and he heard men approaching. Reaching for his knife, he hid behind a nearby tree and waited.

"Father?' It was Hawkeye. "Where are you?"

The Mohican revealed himself and immediately wrapped his arms around his two daring sons, happy to see them alive and unharmed.

"Where are the others?" Uncas inquired, seeing Chingachgook was alone.

Hurriedly their father showed them the long chasm and called out to the others letting them know Hawkeye and Uncas had joined him. The Mohawks were getting closer and there was no more time for talk.

Both Hawkeye and Uncas urged their father to jump next as they took up concealed positions and reloaded their long rifles. Hawkeye spotted a Mohawk and fired, hitting the brave in the stomach. The trailing Mohawks fired back.

Meanwhile Chingachgook had started his own run and nearing the cliff he wished he was much, much younger. As he leapt into air, his lungs ached from the exertion and his progress seemed as slow as a lazy turtle in mud. The other ledge was before him but not below him. Desperately he tried to lean his torso forward and struck the ground in that manner, his stomach slamming into the cliff's lip, his legs dangling in space.

"UGH!" he gasped, his mitten-clad hands trying to gain some purchase.

Both Tamenend and Sagawa had been attempting to revive Kateri when they heard Chingachgook land. Tamenend spun around, saw the Mohican begin to slip over the edge and threw himself forward, hands out.

He was too late; his eyes widened in horror seeing the noble Mohican disappear into the void.

"Go!" Hawkeye cried to Uncas as a hatchet struck the tree behind which he was hiding. The Mohawks, sensing they weren't running any more, had become emboldened and were brazenly coming at them.

"What, and let you have all the fun?"

"And you dare call me stubborn, little brother."

"Go, Hawkeye," Uncas said while ramming another lead ball down his rifle barrel. "Then be prepare to keep these Mohawk dogs from shooting me in the ass."

Visualizing that scene, Nathanial chuckled, moved away from his cover and jogged past his brother, slapping him on his shoulder as he passed.

"Don't be late!"

Having seen his father's run, Hawkeye found the now well-trod lane in the snow and without slowing down, kept running forward.

"Here I come!" he cried as he jumped high to make sure those who had preceded him would be backed away from the ledge, allowing him plenty of room to land.

He came down hard, stumbled forward a few feet and then steadied himself. As he quickly surveyed the area, he saw Kateri sitting up with her back to a boulder, being looked after by Sagawa. Back by the ledge, Tamenend was standing stoically facing him.

"Where is Chingachgook?'

"He did not jump far enough," Tamenend's voice was brittle, the difficult words catching in his throat. "He struck the lip and before I could aid him....fell into...the...pit."

When three shots in a row peppered the clump of rocks Uncas hid behind, he knew it was his time to join his allies. Staying in a low crouch, he moved away from the rocks and wove his way amongst the copse of evergreens to the cleared area that led to the cliff.

Behind him, Kurok, the Mohawk war chief, was berating his braves to keep moving forward. The enemy had stopped firing at them and he thought they were either dead or wounded. Either way, they had to charge or their wily prey would somehow escape them once again and he could not let that happen.

This time they would not be denied their victory.

As the Mohawks charged along, one of them spotted Uncas running beyond the trees.

"Hurry," Kurok shouted.

And as he and his braves rushed forward they beheld the fleeing man suddenly leap into the air and vanish.

Three seconds later they reached the edge of the chasm and came to quick stop.

"He's not dead," Sagawa declared upon hearing Tamenend's words to Hawkeye.

"What do you mean?" Tamenend snapped at the smaller man. "I saw him fall away with my own eyes."

"Yes, I know," Sagawa agreed. "But he's not dead, I tell you." He looked to both Hawkeye and Tamenend, his hands out in supplication.

"How can this be?" Hawkeye was remembering his dream the night before and the ghostly Totten's admonishment, *Listen to Sagawa.* Was this what the dream had meant?

Sagawa moved to Hawkeye and touched his chest. "I do not know how, Hawkeye, but I can sense his spirit. It still lives."

"That's crazy," Tamenend was losing his patience. "How could he…"

The big man stopped talking. Of the three of them, he was the one standing closest to the edge. He turned his head and then took a step towards where the Mohican had fallen away. Dropping to one knee, he leaned over the precipice and heard a voice calling from bellow. "Help me."

Shocked, Tamenend heard the cry a second time. He dropped flat on the ground and looked down.

"What is it?" Hawkeye wanted to know, coming to kneel beside him.

Just then another figure came hurdling through the sky and almost collided with the scout. He dived out of the way just as Uncas came down and rolled to his side.

On his back, the young Mohican looked up at his stepbrother. "What were you trying to do, catch me?"

"It's Chingachgook!" Tamenend exclaimed, still flat on the ground.

Hawkeye forgot Uncas and rushed to the Delaware. "Where?"

"Below. I can't make it out but it looks like he landed on a rock outcropping."

Hawkeye started to drop to his own knees when a war-whoop split the night and he looked across the chasm to see a dozen Mohawks all lined up facing them.

At their center, even in the dark, Hawkeye could distinguish the white part of Kurok's war paint.

Rifles fired and their bullets struck all around the Mohicans and Delawares.

"Take cover!" Hawkeye scrambled away from the ledge, along with Tamenend.

They and others found various boulders to hide behind. At the same time Uncas had finished reloading his rifle.

"Where is father?"

"He didn't make the jump," Hawkeye told him. "He's stuck on a ledge and we have to pull him up."

More rifle slugs whizzed over their heads, smacking into distant trees.

"What about them?" Uncas nodded his head toward the other ledge and the Mohawks.

"We end this contest now," Hawkeye said and then stepped out from behind the round boulder and holding his rifle high over his head, walked to the tip of the cliff.

"Kurok of the Mohawks! It is I, *La Longue Carabine*."

Instantly the shooting stopped from the other side and Uncas shook his head in bewilderment. What was his brother going to do next?

He didn't have long to learn.

"I challenge you to a shooting duel, Kurok. Each of us to face off with our rifles and take one shot."

"You try to trick me, Mohican dog."

"Tell me, Mohawk, have you ever heard that *La Longue Carabine* was not a man of his word? That I am liar and a trickster?"

After a pause, Kurok replied. "No. It is said *La Longue Carabine* is a man of honor."

"Then let us settle this as men of honor and courage. Let us see which is the bravest."

Hawkeye's last words were purposely intended for Kurok's men to hear. He had challenged their war chief and made it impossible for Kurok to decline or else he would forever lose face amongst his people.

"Let it be so," Kurok declared and with hand signals commanded his braves to move away from him. Then holding his own long rifle in his arms he moved to the edge of the cliff and waited.

Hawkeye cradled his own weapon and moved to the edge of the chasm.

"Whenever you are ready, Kurok. We will fire together."

The Mohawk stood like a stone statue.

Hawkeye did the same, while wiggling his trigger finger through the slit in his thick glove. He would only have one chance.

Suddenly Kurok twisted his body and brought his rifle up to his shoulder. Across the gap, Hawkeye mirrored his every action; turning his own body sideways.

The flint struck the powder pan of both rifles and smoke belched from each barrel.

Kurok's shot tore into Hawkeye's left arm, ripping through his heavy leather sleeve causing him to drop his weapon.

At the same time his lead ball struck the Mohawk in the temple and tore off the top of his scalp. Kurok fell over; his body tumbling into the deep well of blackness.

The young Mohawk named Mucha saw Kurok fall at the hands of the Mohican marksman and felt disgust and relief. The entire raid had turned into a disaster that had taken the lives of more than half their number and they had yet to even lay eyes on the Delaware village that had been their destination.

Now his fellow braves clustered together on the cliff and wondered what to do next. Ironically, most of the senior warriors were dead now and Mucha saw that none of his companions knew what do to next.

"This is over," he told them when on one else would speak. "We will return to the caves and there find shelter. Then in the morning we return to our own lands and villages."

When no one disagreed, Mucha looked across to the other plateau and raised up his empty hand in salute. The wounded sharpshooter did the same acknowledging they were of the same mind to end things here and now.

Silently the Mohawks followed Mucha away from the cliff and were soon gone from sight.

The duel over, Uncas and the others rushed to Hawkeye's assistance. Fortunately his thick coat had prevented the lead ball from doing more than tearing off a layer of skin from his arm. For now he allowed Kateri to tear off a piece of his shirt and use it as a bandage around the wound.

His concern was still Chingachgook and how to bring him up safely off the precarious outcropping he was stuck on.

In the end it was Sagawa who once again had the solution. As Chingachgook was beyond arm's reach, he suggested that Tamenend and Uncas lower him by his legs until Chingachgook could grab hold of his arms and use the young man as a ladder and climb to safety.

Hawkeye wasn't sure the idea would work, but in the end it was the only one that they could actually put into action. As he watched his brother and Tamenend take hold of Sagawa's legs and lower him over the lip, he once again marveled at the young man's courage as well as his intelligence. He could see why Totten regarded him so highly.

Minutes later, with much huffing and puffing, Chingachgook appeared over Sagawa's backside and Hawkeye extended his good right arm to him and helped pull him up the remainder of the way.

Once the Mohican was safe, Tamenend and Uncas pulled Sagawa back to safety and all of them sat back to relax and catch their breaths.

"Thank you," Chingachgook said, looking from Sagawa to Tamenend. "The people of the Delewares are fortunate to have such men in their tribe."

It was high praise indeed, one both would remember forever.

"If we're all done patting each other on the back," Uncas complained, "can we get off this mountain and go home now?"

"My son," Chingachgook replied, "that is a very good idea."

One by one the men got to their feet, and with the maid Kateri, started back down the trail towards a new dawn.

Test of Bravery

Frank Schildiner

The spring thaw had begun in the hills surrounding the Hudson River, leaving the land bare but beginning to return to life after the harsh winter. The thick trees were just beginning to bloom and birds and other animals were slowly becoming more visible across the land. Three figures approached a fast moving brook, one bubbling with nearly frozen, clear water newly melted from the nearby mountains. They moved at a quick pace, three men adept at moving through the unbroken wilderness with respcct and thc skill needed to survive on the land.

The oldest of the three men stopped at the brook, pulling out a water skin and immediately began to fill the nearly empty container. He was a powerfully built man, older by many years to his two companions, though with an air of authority that caused most men to listen to his every word. He was Chingachgook, a war chief of the Mohicans and father to both men.

The youngest of the three followed his father to the brook, repeating Chingachgook's actions and filling a second one he always carried in case one of them lost their skin in their travels. He was a tall young man with clear dark skin and ebony hair flowed down his back. Uncas, son of

Chingachgook, possessed a mischievous glint in his eye that caused some to underestimate him in battle. This was a mistake; he was a fierce fighter and a deadly shot with the long rifle that was slung over his shoulder.

The final member of the trio stood a little taller than Uncas, but with a rangier build than both men. His dark hair was almost as black as his adopted father and brother and fell about his shoulders in a tangle. His face was handsome and possessed the weather-beaten skin of one who made the wilderness his home. But most that met this man were struck by the way he seemed to take in every detail around him, not missing anything in his surroundings. Leaning on his long rifle, this was Nathaniel Poe, also known as Hawkeye and Le Longue Carabine, adopted son of Chingachgook, foster brother of Uncas.

Hawkeye was about to step up to the stream when his nose twitched and he slowly began to scan the area. After the scent hit him again, he looked to Chingachgook and said in a low voice, "Father! Smoke!"

Chingachgook frowned and looked about, not smelling anything. But he trusted his adopted son, knowing the latter was one who never raised an alarm without cause. No, this would be no campfire, but something far more dangerous. "Which direction?" he asked, glancing about slowly.

Uncas sniffed the air and shook his head, "I don't smell anything."

Chingachgook chuckled and clapped Uncas on the back, "Your white brother has the nose of a fox. You'll sense it soon enough. We need a better view of the land."

Uncas grinned widely and handed his rifle to his father, moving quickly towards a nearby tree and scrambling up the limbs. Of the three, Uncas was by far the best climber, have the gift of knowing which branches would bear his weight as he ascended to incredible heights.

A moment later he called down in a strong voice, "My brother was right! South some miles away, a large cloud of smoke!"

"There's a settlement that direction, New Hope I believe it is called." Hawkeye replied, looking to the south and frowning at the thought of a large cloud of smoke from that area.

Chingachgook nodded sagely, "Yes, my son. A fire, the great danger to all white settlements. Wooden homes on top of each other, the fire spreads as fast as the deep woods in a dry season."

"Then we go to give them what help we can offer." Hawkeye stated, knowing his adopted father and brother would wish to do the same. That was their way: when people needed aid, they came to assist. It was an unspoken law of those who lived in the wild.

Uncas took his gun, handed Hawkeye the second skin of water he always carried, and off they ran. Their pace was fast but controlled, one they all knew well would carry them vast distances without the need for breaks for rest or food. Hawkeye took the lead, the swiftest of the trio on foot, with Uncas not far behind. Chingachgook followed, his stolid face as expressionless as a boulder as he kept pace with his sons.

Through the woods and hills they ran, their direction set by their knowledge of the land. They seldom spoke as they guided their way through the land, eating and drinking as they navigated the paths known only to a very few who live in harmony with the wilderness. The smell of burning wood grew stronger as they approached, a scent that grew stronger with each mile. But a second smell rose as well, not as strong as that caused by the fire. They all knew that it was one of death, not a natural form of the end of all who lived, but an unclean end caused by the violence of man. This caused them to increase their pace noticeably, knowing they would be needed at the end of their journey.

What would have taken most men a full day to arrive at the settlement, took them merely several hours as they arrived on the outskirts of New Hope. They had visited this location before the winter and knew that the settlement was several small farms and a small church built by the locals. The sight that greeted them was a ruin, the houses and church were no long aflame but smoke still rose from the charred ruins of the church and visible homes. One small barn appeared to still be standing, though scorch marks were visible from the distance.

"They're back!" A man's voice cried, high and loud off to their right. "They're back to kill those of us left alive!"

The trio spun in place towards the source of the yell, spotting a soot stained man with a battered hatchet in hand. He was screaming uncontrollably and running towards Chingachgook with the tool held high above his head. He resembled a man going to war, but it was obvious in the first glance that he'd never attacked another man with a hand weapon before that moment.

The screaming man ran straight for Chingachgook, who stood his ground, appearing almost disinterested in the latter's attack. At the last moment he exploded into action, catching the man's arm as he swung towards the Mohican war chief's head and tossing the man aside. The older warrior stood holding the hatchet, dropping it behind him in a bored gesture.

The fallen man began to scream again when an older white settler, just at soot covered but looking less wild, stopped him with a hand on the other's shoulder. "Hold yourself, Elias! These are not the monsters who attacked us! Don't you recognize them?"

He looked over his shoulder, his face apologetic and continued, "Forgive Elias, please. His home was destroyed and his young wife and son killed. I remember you, good sirs, and know you are all famous for being good men."

"How do we know?" Elias asked, his voice rising as he stood, "How do we know they are not in league with Satan's minions who robbed us of our families and homes?"

"My father could have killed you," Uncas replied, his voice mild but with steel beneath the gentle tone. "Yet he chose not to hurt you when attempted to put an ax in his skull."

Elias stared at Chingachgook, taking in the latter's powerful frame, long rifle and mighty war ax and, even in his fearful state, recognized the truth. He rose, looking shamefaced and lost, unable to make eye contact with anyone.

"We were attacked in the early morning hours," the older man, who turned out to be named William Johnson, explained. "A war party, they were screaming and lighting homes on fire. They killed anyone they could and ran away into the night."

"Why?" Hawkeye asked, spotting the newly dug graves and the survivors attempting to find a means of comprehending the attack. "This attack makes no sense. Most of your animals are still here and they took no prisoners."

"How did you know that?" William asked, clearly confused by Hawkeye's reasoning. But he answered the former's question soon enough. "They attacked us to harm all settlers who try and make a life here. The Mohawks aren't far away. We think they're out to kill all English."

Chingachgook shook his head slowly, "No. The Iroquois League of Six Nations made peace with the English. To break that treaty would cause the five other tribes to rise against them in battle. My white son speaks the truth. This was the act of renegades."

William shrugged, accepting their reasoning easily, "I trust you are correct. That makes sense to me."

"But not to me," Hawkeye replied, some force in his tone. "Renegade bands seek to steal from white and Indian alike. They seek horses, weapons, food, cattle, and women. They do not just run in, burn people out and flee into the darkness. Something strange is at work here."

"Agreed," Chingachgook stated with a nod, "We should speak to the Mohawk. The renegades may have scattered to the winds. Best to find out why they attack first."

Only Hawkeye and Uncas knew how impressive a gesture this was for the Mohican war chief to take for these people. Chingachgook had battled the Mohawk on many occasions in his life and for him to willingly embrace the recent peace between their peoples was an act of true honor. Many on both sides refused to release the anger of past battles and loss and wished to continue on the path of blood. But Chingachgook held true to his own word as well as that of his people and he raised his sons in the same manner.

"Gather your people and animals and begin to rebuild," Hawkeye advised, looking down at William. His dark eyes seemed to bore into the English settler, causing the smaller man to straighten and listen intently. "We will track down the renegades and inform you when it is complete. Oh, and share all your goods, let no one go hungry, thirsty or cold."

The last statement was made in a raised voice, causing all of the survivors to listen and a few to nod their heads. The European love of land ownership would be a hindrance this day and could result in the deaths of those who lost everything in attack. The way of Chingachgook's people, living in harmony with the land and all working to keep every member of the group from suffering, was the only way these settlers would survive another week.

After filling their skins with water from the still working well, the trio were off, heading west towards the Mohawk tribal lands. They knew, with the day already on the wane, that they would not reach the encampment this evening, but wished to gain as much distance as they could before nightfall. They traveled, as they always did, swiftly and cautiously, men raised in this lands and knowing every possible danger that could confront them on a journey.

Just before nightfall Uncas spotted a turkey and brought the large bird down with one shot. That was their way, "one shot, one kill," and they would take no more than they needed to survive. A short time later they stopped and made camp, building a fire and cleaning and cooking the turkey for their meal. As they waited for the bird to finish cooking, Chingachgook moved to the edge of the clearing, his dark eyes staring off into the darkness.

Hawkeye moved to his side and, for a time, they stood in a companionable silence. Finally the younger man asked, "Something disturbs you, father?"

Chingachgook did not answer for a time, continuing to look ahead and see things either in the darkness or within his own mind. "The white man who attacked me, Elias. He was ready to condemn all men who resembled me. Because my skin is darker than his and I dress in the skins of leather."

Hawkeye first thought to excuse the terrified man who lost his family, but he knew that would be a lie. There were many who viewed the men and women of the tribes as less than human, animals who sought to burn them out of their homes and steal their property. This was a falsehood since few of the tribes could comprehend the idea of owning land and not caring for it as one would the mother who brought you life.

"The English and French, they love to own land and other baubles. They believe it makes them wealthy and important," Hawkeye stated, repeating what he'd learned from his father over the years and what he'd observed when dealing with European settlers.

Chingachgook exhaled loudly in agreement, "I fear that will mean the end of my people. Because the whites' greed for land and building farms and settlements, excluding even their own people, will only grow in time. Fighting back will only delay the future and possibly make the world a worse place."

Hawkeye wished he could offer some words of encouragement, telling his father that the future of their people need not be so bleak. But he didn't believe the old man was wrong. Greed, no matter your skin color, destroyed lives. The European love of taking lands and using them without regards for others or the future was a disease, one that did not seem to have any cure. It would be a sad day when settlements and roads replaced the woods and animals of this land, but there seemed no way to prevent that bleak time from happening one day.

After a time, standing together in the darkness, they rejoined Uncas at the fire and ate. Before long they turned in for the night, sleeping peacefully under the stars, knowing a day like none other lay before them in the Mohawk camp.

The Mohawk camp was a new one, having been built before the winter snows, and would not be used much longer. The Mohawk, like many of the tribes, did not linger in one location for fear of using the land up and making it useless to all. Scouts spotted the two Mohicans and their white companion several miles away, watching them closely and realizing their intent was to head for the Mohawk lands. Hawkeye, Chingachgook and Uncas spotted the scouts easily, but were careful to make no threatening moves to alarm them in any way. This was difficult; all three had fought

Mohawk on many occasions and the recent peace, thanks to the English, was still hard to comprehend at times. Previously the Mohawk were allied with the French and for many years fought the Mohicans and others in small battles.

"Hold!" A powerful voice called to them when they were within a mile of the Mohawk encampment. "What brings two Mohicans and a white man to Mohawk lands?"

A tall warrior stepped from the trees, a man older than Hawkeye or Uncas but not Chingachgook. He was ramrod straight, with the burly physique of a bear. In his hands he held a large war club and a musket, the gun being new and obviously of English make. His head was free of hair except for a tuft at the back of his head, from which three braids fell across his shoulders. This was the Mohawk way, they plucked their skull clean except for the back of their head, which they then grew in braids.

Chingachgook stepped forward, raising a hand in greeting, "I am Chingachgook of the Mohicans and these are my sons. We have come to your lands because a white settlement to the east was attacked."

The tall Mohawk stiffened slightly, his eyes flashing, "And you blame us for the attack, Mohican?" he asked, his voice low.

Chingachgook shook his head, "No, but the whites will do so if we do not find out why these renegades attacked their lands."

The Mohawk warrior stared for a moment and then smiled slightly, "I believe you have a story to tell. No," he raised a hand to stop them from speaking, "do not tell me. You would only have to repeat your words when you reached the Chief and his mate. I will send a messenger up ahead and will accompany you to our lands."

"We thank you," Hawkeye replied, impressed that this warrior was willing to take them at their word.

"I have heard of the Mohican war chief, his son and his white son. French and English say you all are true men to your word. With the new peace, I will hope these stories to be true. I am Matanga, which means sage of adviser in English."

"You earn your name well," Chingachgook stated, also impressed by the words of the Mohawk warrior.

"We shall see soon enough. Our chief is named Chinmay, which means 'full of knowledge' in English and his mate is Rajata, which means 'silver.' I explain this to you because the women of the Mohawks have as much right to rule as the men. Many outsiders ignore them at their own peril. Speak fair to them both," Matanga explained as he waved his scouting part out from hiding. He gave quick instructions in the Mohawk language to a young warrior, who left at a run a moment later.

"Your women have a say in council?" Uncas asked, "That is interesting. Women do see the universe different from men."

Matanga, seeing the young warrior was not mocking the Mohawk way, agreed with a smile, "And they often see things we miss. The English lawmakers learned that soon enough!"

With that, they all took off at a quick pace, Matanga and his men leading the visiting trio through paths that lead them towards the Mohawk encampment. None spoke, but there seemed to be little tension since the Mohawk warriors realized their former enemies were not blaming them for an attack which they had no part of this time.

The Mohawk encampment proved to be a little larger than the nearby English settlement, with lodges built in a semi-circular pattern. They were well-spaced from each other and a larger long house was being built at the far end of the clearing. Having heard that a Mohican and his sons, especially an adopted white son, were coming to speak to the chief in peace, the whole encampment appeared to be out watching their approach. Life still went on, men and women worked while children played, but they were all performing these acts with an eye towards the approach of Matanga's hunting party.

Chinmay proved to be an older man, his braids of hair all white and his face creased with lines. His dark eyes were bright and alive with intelligence and he was just beginning to bend with age. His mate Rajata was a tiny woman, doll-like in looks with large bright eyes and a wide smile that was merry and thick dark braids streaked with gray. They were joined by a young girl possibly twenty years old and almost as tall as Chinmay. She was dressed in a leather skirt and jacket and had her thick dark hair twisted into two braids that fell down her back. Her face was heart shaped and her wide mouth was also smiling, though there was a trace of amusement in that greeting.

"I am Dhanyata, niece of Chinmay. He asked me to this council to translate for my aunt who only speaks our language and some French," the girl stated in greeting, nodding to each of the trio. Her eyes lingered a little longer on Uncas and she was smiling a little more after she looked away from the tall Mohican warrior.

"I am Chingachgook, a war chief of the Mohicans. My sons and I greet you in peace and hope you can help us," Chingachgook stated, straightening slightly as he addressed the chief and his mate. He was careful to make eye contact with both, remembering Matanga's warning about ignoring females among the Mohawk.

"I have heard of the war chief Chingachgook, his son and his white son known as La Longue Carabine," Chinmay replied. "You have fought our people in the past yet you hold to the peace. There is honor in that."

"Is there?" A warrior snarled, pushing forward. He was as tall as Matanga yet of thinner build, giving the impression of impressive speed and agility in his movements. He had several scars on his face and body, a nose twisted by multiple breaks and was missing several teeth. The nearby Mohawk all looked at him with distaste, giving him room to stand on his own.

"That is Meghana, which means raincloud," Matanga explained, sounding resigned as the other warrior stepped forward. "He was a great warrior during the many battles with the English and our enemies. But he has no taste for the peace. Meghana looks for war everywhere now."

Meghana looked over Chingachgook, Uncas and Hawkeye with open disgust, staring at them for several heartbeats before he rasped, "The tales of the great warrior, his son and his adopted white pet are sad stories of children. You come to the Mohawk to make us look poor in the eyes of all."

"No!" Uncas yelled, "We come because an English settlement was attacked by raiders, renegades!"

"You call us raiders, killers of children and attackers upon the weak?" Chinmay asked, his voice mild. But there was a tension in the air as everyone waited for the answer.

"No," Hawkeye replied, leaning on his rifle. "We came for your help. The English will accuse you of the attack if the renegades are not found. We don't want to break the new peace or have your people condemned for foolish acts."

"Lies!" Meghana snapped back, moving closer, "The white man lies! He and his Mohican followers seek to make us look like fools in the eyes of the whites! I think you did the attack on the whites and seek to blame us!"

Uncas pushed forward, his face twisted with anger, but was held back by a restraining hand from Chingachgook. The older warrior looked Meghana up and down with open revulsion and asked in a deliberately mild voice, "Is this how men are treated who come to you in peace?"

"Do you come in peace, old teller of tales? I have heard how this white man killed four Mohawk braves by himself and never misses a deer he shoots. These are lies, told by the treacherous dogs who seek our deaths. I challenge anyone to defy my words!" Meghana roared, lifting his arms up above his head as he spoke.

Hawkeye stepped forward, his face impassive, "I am Nathaniel Poe, known as Hawkeye and La Longue Carabine, adopted son of Chingachgook of the Mohicans. And I accept your challenge, Meghana of the Mohawks!"

Meghana's scarred face twisted into a wide rictus of a grin. It was an ugly look, one filled with malice, cruelty and anger, a visage that would horrify all but the bravest men in the world. But Hawkeye and his adopted father and brother were not intimidated. If anything, this strengthened their resolve.

"Then it shall be a challenge of bravery. And Meghana will show the white to be a coward and a lowly lying dog," Meghana said, his voice barely above a whisper.

"So be it," Chinmay replied, sounding resigned. "Take our visitors to my lodge as the grounds are prepared. Bring them food and drink and let them rest."

"Follow me," Matanga stated, his expression stony. He led them to a large lodge and invited them inside, taking a seat beside them and waiting until food and water were provided. When they were alone again, he spoke, "Meghana sought to insult you. I apologize for my people."

"It was not your doing, Matanga," Hawkeye said, shaking his head. "Does Meghana always seek to start battles with strangers?"

Matanga shook his large head slowly, clearly confused, "No, that is not his way in battle. He prefers to wait until someone is vulnerable or unaware. Then he pounces and strikes them with the speed of a bolt of lightning. This behavior is unexpected. Now I must leave you and see that the grounds for the bravery test are ready."

"What is a bravery test to the Mohawk, father?" Uncas asked, thinking of the girl, Dhanyata. She was very pretty and seemed braver than most girls he'd met in his time.

Chingachgook drank deeply from his bowl of water and explained, "I have heard of this test from a Huron who endured it once. They soak a large fallen tree in water and lay it across a pit. In the pit they place kindling and fire it. The two challengers stand on the log and are given a stick. They may strike the other, one blow at a time, as the flames grow higher and higher. The first to flee the log is declared the loser and is often beaten quite badly by the men and women of the village."

"But even a wet log will eventually take flame! What is to prevent both from falling and burning to death?" Uncas asked, amazed by this test.

"Nothing, my son," Chingachgook explained, sounding resigned. "It has been said that those without the sense to know fear will eventually throw themselves into a flame to prove the fire does not frighten them. The Mohawks know this all too well. But I believe there is more to this test."

"I agree," Hawkeye replied, frowning. "Meghana was too anxious to keep us here and insult us. He seeks to delay us or stop our search for the renegades."

"You think he is one of their number?" Uncas asked, seeing his father and brother's reasoning now.

"I think that will prove true," the elder Mohican war chief stated, picking up his war club and checking it over. "But we will have a hard time proving such a story. He is Mohawk and we are outsiders."

Uncas shook his head. "He may be their blood, but they are not proud to call him one of their tribe. They look at him the way most would a poisonous snake."

"Agreed," Hawkeye said, giving his brother a smile, "and that is why I will fight him in this bravery test. By not insulting him or the Mohawk, he had no choice but to take me on in some challenge. This one is as fair as I could hope for in a former enemy encampment."

"I had hoped he would challenge me to a duel with war clubs. But he would not be able to speak after I crushed his skull," Chingachgook added with a dry chuckle.

The testing grounds were a short distance from the Mohawk encampment. A pit, probably dug for waste, was aflame and men and women were adding logs to the fire to causing the flames to slowly rise. Hawkeye stripped off his jacket and shirt, handing them to Uncas, along with his rifle and other weapons. Finally he removed his boots, knowing they might become slippery on the now wet log.

Matanga approached and handed Hawkeye a thin stick, little longer than a man's arm. "Chinmay will call out each time you can strike. No attacks to the eyes or between the legs are allowed. Strike either and you will be declared the loser. Push your opponent or strike him with anything but the stick will also show you lack bravery and you will be the loser of the contest. Fall into the pit and you will die, none will save you."

"I understand," Hawkeye replied, taking the weapon and watching across the pit. Meghana stood there, a smaller man at his side speaking to the warrior and making fast gestures with his hands. "Matanga? Who stands there with Meghana?"

"That is Meghana only friend, Yed, which means sacred knowledge. He is a coward who pretends to listen to the shaman of our tribe. But truly he does so because he is afraid of blood and battle. Yed lied for Meghana several times when we were children and has followed him ever since that time. A sad nothing of a man," Matanga explained. He gave them a nod and walked off.

They were soon joined by Dhanyata, who smiled openly at Uncas and looked over Hawkeye with grave eyes. "My uncle is sorry you were forced to prove your honesty and bravery. Even when we were your enemy, none ever called you three liars or cowards."

"Thank you," Hawkeye replied and gave his head a quick shake, indicating that he wished to speak to Chingachgook before the battle began. They took several steps away and Hawkeye said in a low voice, "I think the girl has eyes for my brother."

Chingachgook smiled briefly in agreement, but said, "But that is not why you wished to speak to me alone, my son."

Hawkeye knew better than to be surprised by his father's ability to see the truth of a situation, no matter how dire. "Yes. My concern is this Yed. If he is Meghana's only follower, then he may attempt to turn the trial against me. Beware of treachery on his part."

Before Chingachgook could reply, Chinmay was heard to call out, "Challengers, step forward. The trial shall begin."

Chingachgook gripped his adopted son's arm tight for a moment and moved off into the shadows. Soon he was barely visible, moving in the near darkness as silent as a fox and far more deadly. Uncas gave his brother a wide smile, Dhanyata at his side. Hawkeye grinned back and turned towards the testing ground, his face immediately impassive as he stepped forward. Soon the battle would begin and he focused on what he knew of Meghana.

Meghana stepped towards the log, looked down at the fire and whooped loudly, his face twisting again into his horrific rictus grin. He danced several steps and pointed his stick at Hawkeye, calling out in Mohawk and screaming incomprehensible sounds like a man in a frenzy. Hawkeye was unimpressed, knowing instantly this was a ruse on Meghana's part to either frighten him or make him drop his guard. The whooping and hollering was in hopes that Hawkeye would be terrified by the "crazed savage," the bizarre behavior was in case he was not frightened, Meghana hoped Hawkeye would see him as a lunatic who would be easy to defeat. No, Matanga was right, Meghana was a dangerous, cunning warrior who tried to make opponents drop their guard so they would be easier to defeat in battle.

Stepping onto the log at the same time as his enemy, Hawkeye looked unconcerned, almost bored by the ritual test of bravery that was about to begin. Meghana looked startled by the white man's lack of reaction to his antics. The few times he demanded a bravery test, he was able to frighten his enemies before the battle and win before a blow was struck. But this adopted white son of Mohican war chief appeared as if Meghana was merely an ant hill he needed to step over so he could get to more interesting game. Odd, but Meghana thought that too might be a ruse and the white man was putting up a good front to hide his fears.

"Yes," Meghana thought as he moved to the center of the log, "that is probably the reason for his calm. But if not, Yed will see the white dog reaches his grave soon enough."

The heat for both warriors standing on the log was close to unbearable, rising with each second and causing them to immediately become drenched with sweat. Young boys and girls were feeding logs into the fire and causing the flames to slowly grow. Within minutes the log they stood upon would be alight and it wouldn't be long before both men were in peril of dying a terrible death.

"Strike!" Chinmay called out, his voice rising above the chatter of Mohawks speaking as both warriors stood atop the flaming log.

Meghana whooped loud and swung his stick in a fast arc towards Hawkeye's front leg. He knew most attacked the head and body, but the Mohawk warrior always believed if you crippled a man's legs they would be unable to fight before long. This had served him in battle many times, causing the death of anyone he considered an enemy. Even a few Mohawk fell to his attacks this way and he was able to blame their deaths on the Huron or the Mohicans.

But Meghana's favorite attack was immediately apparent to Hawkeye, sensing this man was more like a vulture than a wolf. He would happily wait until a man was weak with fatigue rather than face him fresh, would mutilate a dead body of those he considered an enemy, rather than show respect to a fallen opponent. Such a man would wish to weaken his enemy in his attack, make the fight easier and the end one in which he can bring slowly and with the most cruelty possible.

Which was why Hawkeye brought his stick down and blocked Meghana's attack. Trained by his adopted father Chingachgook in the ways of the war club and other weapons, he knew all too well how an attack on a man's legs could be the death of even the strongest warrior. And, knowing that Meghana was at heart a cruel man who wished to see his enemies in agony before he granted them a slow and lingering death, Hawkeye looked for an attack to either his legs or eye.

Happily his belief in Meghana's ways proved correct and he stopped the blow mere inches from his left leg. Seeing the Mohawk warrior's look of surprise, Hawkeye gave him a slight smile, denoting that he knew what the cruel brave planned to do with his attacks.

The assembled Mohawks *oohed* with surprise, at Hawkeye's action, impressed that instead of attacking he countered Meghana and seemed unconcerned by the latter's actions. As the youths fed the fire, many moved a little closer to the contest, wondering how this test of bravery would end. But all did have to admit, the adopted son of a former enemy did appear to have a great deal of courage and bravery.

"Strike!" Chinmay called again, secretly hoping Hawkeye performed bravely. The new treaty with the English was a path he considered an honorable one and having a white behave with bravery would prove his point: that they need not be enemies; that the path of war resulted in no true victors in the end.

Meghana screamed high and loud leaping forward and swinging for Hawkeye's shoulder. A small strike to the collar bone was another attack he loved; rob an enemy of an arm as well as cause him an enormous amount of pain and victory would soon follow. But Hawkeye was ready for this attack too, swinging his stick up and striking Meghana's wrist. The Mohawk warrior's hand involuntarily opened and the stick fell from his grasp, falling into the fire.

Staring in shock at his now empty hand, Meghana stepped back, his twisted features frozen in a look of terror and rage. The white man outfought him, treating the Mohawk warrior as if he was a child that needed to be taught a lesson rather than a fellow brave. Meghana swore revenge, determined to make this man and his adopted family die in the worst and most horrific way possible. But before that time, Yed would no doubt prevent this man from harming Meghana.

There was a cry of pain off in the twilight, one ignored by all. So intent were they by the coming attack by Hawkeye, more than a few of the Mohawk men and women were startled when Chinmay again stated, "Strike!"

Hawkeye smiled, stepped forward and tossed his stick into the fire. He crossed his arms across his chest, hearing the rumble of surprise and confusion from all present. He made no move to advance or attack further, but merely stood sweating as the flames leapt around him, growing hotter with each second that passed.

"Why do you not strike?" Chinmay asked, as surprised as all of the other members of his tribe by the adopted son of the Mohicans and his actions.

Hawkeye, keeping his eyes on the hunched and staring Meghana, replied, "I do not attack an unarmed man. My father, Chingachgook, war chief of the Mohicans, raised me to be honorable to friends and enemies alike. Let the test of bravery continue, I will stand here as will Meghana and we will see who flees for safety first."

Chinmay smiled and nodded slowly, "The test will continue until one falls in or flees or both die. That is the way of this trial."

Hawkeye smiled across at Meghana, who was clearly sweating from more than the growing heat. The flames were just beginning to lick the bottom of the tree they stood upon and the heat was growing more and more and would unbearable in a short time. But Hawkeye stood still, willing himself to ignore the cinders that were being tossed into the air and causing small burns to his unshod feet. No, this was the way to defeat Meghana and earn the respect of the Mohawk. Then they could find out who was behind the renegade attack on the settlement of New Hope.

Meghana stood as far as he knew he was allowed on the log, wondering why Yed had not acted. This was the time to strike the white man and cause him to fall into the flames. None of the assembled tribe would spot their way of guaranteeing Meghana's victory and none would mourn the death of a former enemy. As to the Mohican war chief and his son, they would die soon enough and their screams of agony would be the best music to his ears. But for now he waited and planned to beat Yed for prolonging this battle so long.

Hawkeye watched Meghana, seeing the man's terror grow with each moment. Both knew it would not be much longer before the bottom of the log was alight, the soaking water having long since burned off by the heat and flame. The Mohawk warrior would break soon, that much was clear. But all Hawkeye could do was wait and pray that his beliefs about Meghana still proved true.

Seeing the bottom portion of the tree catch fire was the breaking point for Meghana, the point where his fears overwhelmed his ability to hide his true nature. He knew, deep in his heart, that he was a coward. Men like Matanga stood in the place of honor in battle charging forward with little regard as to whether they would survive. Meghana pretended to do so but always looked for the weakness in those he attacked, unwilling to risk fighting an equal or greater warrior. His kills were higher than most Mohawks, but some, like Matanga, regarded him as a lesser being. Even this bravery test was planned to guarantee his victory. If the attacks failed then Yed would secretly cause the white man to fall. Yet none of this was happening!

With a scream born of terror and anger, Meghana pulled out a long bladed hunting knife and charged Hawkeye. He always kept the blade strapped to his leg in case he needed to suddenly kill someone and was not near his favorite war club. A cry of surprise rose among the Mohawk, shocked that one of their own would so clearly violate the rules of the bravery test. This was a humiliation to the tribe, especially in the face of a former enemy like the Mohican and his son!

Hawkeye was as surprised by the appearance of a knife as anyone present, but he quickly weighed his options. Retreating would risk his falling into the fire and dying in agony. But not retreating would mean he was being attacked by a crazed Mohawk warrior with a knife. Neither was a good choice, but there was little else to do at this moment.

Meghana slashed out, his speed impressive and Hawkeye was barely able to back a bit and get out of the way of the wicked steel. He knew the Mohawk warrior would stick to small quick attacks; they favored him and would soon result in severe injury or death for Hawkeye. Backing another step and causing Meghana to grin madly, Hawkeye suddenly stepped in close and punched the Mohawk warrior in his flattened nose. He followed that strike with a quick kick to the man's shin, causing Meghana to shriek in pain and drop his knife. He was about to tip over and fall into the leaping flames, when Hawkeye grabbed the Mohawk warrior by the arm and pulled them both to safety.

The cool grass was a comfort as Hawkeye stumbled to the ground and he noted that Uncas was suddenly by his side. His adopted brother lifted a water skin to his lips, urging him to drink slowly and stay seated on the ground. Dhanyata was by Uncas's side, her face a little drawn as she watched the two men closely.

Chinmay appeared a moment later, waving for Hawkeye to remain seated as he tried to rise. "Why did you save Meghana? That was an act of bravery few would undertake," he asked, watching the white son of the Mohicans with close attention.

Hawkeye cleared his throat and took another small sip of the water, "I never sought his death. I kill only when I have no choice. Also I believe Meghana knows more than he says about the renegades who attacked the white settlement of New Hope."

Chinmay cocked his head, surprised by the latter part of the answer, "You accuse us of treachery?"

Uncas shook his and and spoke for them both, "Only Meghana, not the rest of the Mohawk people."

"You lie!" Meghana snarled, trying to lunge forward but was restrained by several strong hands. He knew his position was a bad one. Attacking with a knife in a bravery test was a violation of his people's way. But if he kept to his story, that the white man and his Mohicans were merely there to sow seeds of mistrust, then he might survive. "You must have attacked the whites and are trying to make us the victims of your acts!"

"Hold your lying tongue, you dog!" Matanga roared as he stepped forward, Chingachgook at his side. The huge Mohawk warrior tossed Yed to the ground at Chinmay's feet and stated, "The Mohican and I caught Meghana's follower as he attempted to attack the white man in the test. This explains how Meghana defeated two others in bravery tests. Their falls always confused me!"

Matanga tossed a sling, one that all of the tribe knew Yed used to catch rabbits and other small animals to prove he was a hunter as well as a shaman. He proved to be a small, sallow faced man with the hunched shoulders of a whipped dog and tiny eyes that never seemed to stop moving. To Hawkeye the man named Yed resembled a large rat dressed in the skins of a Mohawk man. He seemed the perfect follower for a nasty character like Meghana.

"I didn't! I saw a rabbit and was going to hit it for my dinner!" Yed wailed, his voice a pitiable whine that made his resemblance to a rat all the more real to those who watched him in the light of the fire pit.

Matanga laughed, a harsh sound that didn't possess a trace of humor in it, "You would go hunting rabbits while your only friend fought a trial of bravery against the white son of a Mohican man? I think not, Yed!"

Chinmay stepped forward, hearing the murmurs of anger forming among his people. He would not allow his tribe to fall on Meghana and Yed, despite their obvious guilt. But there was a larger tale hidden here and he would find out the truth. The way to that was to confirm Matanga's tale and then he could discover what the two evil men were concealing from his people at this time.

"Matanga," Chinmay began, his voice calm and clear, "How did you know Yed would act with evil in his heart?"

"Chingachgook and his adopted white son believed treachery was afoot with these two curs. To prevent it, our new Mohican ally asked me stand with him and watch Yed. I saw as Yed pulled out his sling and a small stone, and was about to throw it at the white man. I stopped him and we brought him before you when the trial was complete," Matanga explained and many, even those who suspected the white man and the Mohicans, of being liars, nodded their approval. None believed Matanga would suddenly lie for two men he barely knew and once fought as an enemy.

"And we all saw Meghana pull out the knife and attack my brother! And my white brother still let him live to receive the justice of your people," Uncas stated, his voice as clear and as strong as Matanga's and Chinmay's and carrying great force with the assembled Mohawks. Hawkeye, and no doubt Chingachgook, observed with some amusement the look of strong approval on the face of Dhanyata as she watched Uncas speak.

"I hear truth in your words," Chinmay replied and looked at the fallen Yed. He now completely believed that Meghana and Yed had knowledge of this attack on the white settlement not far from the Mohawk lands. "Tell us of the renegades. Is Meghana their leader? Or merely a follower?"

"I…I…do not…" Yed stammered as he looked at the restrained Meghana. His friend could not protect him now, but Yed did not want to tell the truth for fear of punishment as well.

"We have a fire already," Matanga said, his voice quiet and deadly. "Let us lower this one into the fire a few times so that we can awaken his tongue."

"Nȯ, please!" Yed wailed, seeing the look of fury on Meghana's face. "Please! Show mercy!"

Matanga lifted Yed from the ground, holding him so his feet barely touched the earth. "Then talk, coward! Tell the truth of these renegades and raiders of women and children. Now!"

"Hold your lying tongue!" Meghana screamed, trying to break free but finding even more hands holding him still. He stopped struggling, knowing his time to escape would come soon enough. He would not stay a prisoner for long!

"Speak truth and I will give you your life," Chinmay added, stepping next to the powerful Matanga and meeting Yed's eye. You will leave our people and no longer be one of our tribe, but you will have life and even some food and water on your journey."

Yed stared at Chinmay and then the giant Matanga and quailed. Even Meghana could not protect him now. But with life there was always a chance to survive and find prosperity another day. And there were other people who might welcome him as an enemy of the Mohawk. That, even more than the thought of torture by the fire, an act Mohawks never did to prisoners, made Yed's mind up for him and he nodded. Matanga lowered the ratlike man to the ground, but stood nearby, his large hands balled into fists.

"A French officer approached us just before the peace. He knew Meghana hated the white English and the idea of peace with the other tribes. Meghana was a scout for him and they got on well when they fought the French enemies. The officer, Captain Albert Dutourd, decided to destroy the peace. He gathered together men who had no tribe any longer and Mohawks like Meghana who hated the English. They attacked three settlements and killed many whites," Yed explained, his voice quavery as he stared at the clearly enraged Matanga. He knew it was only Chinmay's promise that kept the giant warrior from attacking him here and now.

Chinmay looked at Meghana and shook his head, "You would condemn us to war with the English? And the other tribes we are brothers to in the Iroquois League? Why? Do you love blood and battle so much that you would risk all of our deaths?"

Meghana knew it was useless to lie now. That foolish coward Yed had told enough to prove they were both guilty. But there were some who hated the League and the English as much as he did. Best to try and appeal to them now, "We have become weak, bowing to the tribes of the Iroquois League and the English! They seek to make us cowards who are afraid to control our own lands! I would kill every English in the world if it means we can continue to be Mohawk!"

Chinmay shook his head again, his expression mournful, "Meghana, you do not know the Mohawk way. You are a lover of blood and the murder of the weak. I will not sentence you now, your crimes must be heard by my brother and sister chiefs and we will all decide your fate. For now, place him in his lodge and he is not to leave. Take his weapons and have no man or woman speak Meghana's name, for he has shamed us all. Take him away!"

"Hold!" Chingachgook called, his hand above his head, "I would hear from Meghana or his dog where the French man and his band of killers hide!"

Matanga stepped next to Chingachgook and raised his hand as well. "I would know as well! This French man would seek to bring the anger of the English on the Mohawk and I will stand in battle with the Mohican and his sons."

All eyes turned to Meghana, but the twisted-faced man merely laughed and spat on the ground in defiance. They then turned towards Yed and the little ratlike man withered under the collective gaze that condemned him in their eyes. "Five leagues to the north, a large deep cave near the mountains."

"How many men are in this band?" Hawkeye asked, standing and feeling a little better now.

"Twenty," Yed replied, his head hanging. "They have a few English muskets stolen from the soldiers in the fort."

"I believe him," Matanaga said and waved to the warriors to take Yed away. He would be released in the morning, with only some food and water for his journey. He was a Mohawk no longer, but they were not a cruel people and sending a man, even one who betrayed them, into the wilderness without any supplies was an act they would not consider.

"Take Meghana to his lodge and hold him there. He is not to leave and will be fed and given water and nothing else," Chinmay added and watched for a moment as the warrior was dragged away, spitting curses and swearing revenge upon all as he was dragged back towards the encampment.

Turning sad eyes on Chingachgook, Hawkeye and Uncas, Chinmay continued, "You behaved with honor and we thank you. You have revealed a wolf hidden in our people, one who would cause death and misery should his vision be followed. Tomorrow morning, at first light, you will join us in the hunt for the French officer and his followers."

"My father, brother and I will go ahead of your war party," Hawkeye declared. "We travel lighter and faster and will be able to move without being seen or heard. A war party is a noisy band that would alert the Frenchman that we are coming and seek battle."

Chinmay looked as if he was about to argue, when Matanga place a hand on his chief's shoulder. "They have earned this right. La Longue Carabine, his adopted father and brother have proven worthy of our respect."

Chinmay lifted a hand in acknowledgment. "It is agreed. If you require food, water or anything else we can provide, speak the words. The Mohawk will not forget your service to our tribe for many lifetimes."

"Food, water and a place to sleep, soon. Very soon," Hawkeye said, smiling and swaying a little on his feet, causing the assembled warriors to laugh with their new ally. The trial of bravery was a difficult one and the few who took the test could rarely walk, let alone make jokes!

Laughing with the others, Chinmay lead them back to the encampment, issuing orders that their guests be treated well. No longer were they viewed with suspicion by the men, women and children of the Mohawk encampment. The former enemies proved they would be good allies in the future.

In his lodge, Meghana listened as the encampment's noises slowly lessened until only the sounds of insects and the occasional animal could be heard in the distance. By not fighting, he'd been able to fool his guards into believing they needn't worry about his agreeing to remain a prisoner. One guard stood on the door of his small lodge, obviously bored with his duty already. Pulling out the second war club he always kept beneath his blankets, Meghana crept up on the man and struck him hard on the back of his head. The guard was too shocked to cry out and Meghana dragged him into the lodge. Striking the man three more times in the face, he stripped the corpse of his weapons, which proved to be an elderly French musket, a hatchet and a small knife. Meghana stole into the night. He knew a faster path to the cave Dutourd used as an assembly point for his men.

As he ran through the night, Meghana didn't spare a glance for his former people. The Mohawk were becoming weak; just look at how easily he'd killed the warrior meant to guard him this night! Once the Frenchman and his band killed the white man and the two Mohicans, they would rampage through the white settlements and pave a path in blood among the English. The whites would blame the Mohawk and the other nearby tribes and soon there would be battle in every land. This was the future Meghana welcomed, no peace but everyone fighting and killing and he would be one of the leaders in this battle. It was a glorious thought.

Chuckling to himself, he ran through paths he knew all too well, preparing to warn his French friend so they could destroy the enemies who came at his heels…

"Meghana has escaped!" Uncas burst into the lodge as Hawkeye was pulling on his shirt and Chingachgook was checking his weapons a final time. It was just before first light and they were preparing to leave the Mohawk encampment. The war party would soon follow their path.

"How?" Hawkeye demanded, pulling on his shirt and picking up his gear.

Uncas sighed, "He attacked his guard and murdered him in the night. He has several hours at least ahead of us. The Frenchman will know we are coming."

"He will expect a war party, not three men," Chingachgook replied, standing. "And we will follow his path. He will lead us the fastest way to his allies."

Hawkeye nodded and grinned as they stepped from the lodge, unsurprised by the angry voices of men and women as they moved through the growing crowd. At the center stood Matanga, his huge hands balled into fists with fury.

"We will hunt this beast down. Meghana is no man, he is an animal!" Matanga snarled.

Hawkeye shook his head. "Animals do not traitorously kill their own in the night. No, he is more like the men who seek to steal lands, greedy and evil. But my father, brother and I will leave. Follow our tracks and you will find your enemy!"

And with that declaration, all three men were off, their pace slow for a time as they searched for Meghana's spoor. Fortunately a man in the darkness, even one who knows his lands well, cannot hide his path. Soon they were on the run, able to cross vast stretches of space with the speed of deer or other quick animals of the forests. They knew they would not catch Meghana before he reached the cave the French army officer used as a base, but they doubted he would believe they would arrive so close on his heels. Few could traverse the lands of the wild with the speed that Chingachgook, Hawkeye and Uncas could manage with ease.

Hawkeye called a halt when they were on the edge of the mountain region, knowing their speed would no longer help them against the Frenchman and his band. A fast pace was good for moving across distances, but the noise they created was easy to hear at a distance. Now they would need the stealth of hunters, a skill all three excelled in and had used in battle many times in the past.

"I smell a cook fire," Uncas stated, his voice low. "Not far from here."

Hawkeye smiled in agreement. "I smell it too, to the north. Very recent."

All three moved slowly forward until Hawkeye held up a hand to stop their passage. Pointing ahead to their left, Chingachgook and Uncas immediately spotted a guard seated in the distance on a boulder. He was lighting a pipe filled with tobacco and had a large musket across his lap. They studied him for a moment and Chingachgook was the first to speak up.

"Huron," he pronounced in a whisper. "His shirt and legs have their markings. And the Huron are friends to the French to this day. We have found the renegades."

Uncas frowned, "We cannot shoot that man. A shot will tell his friends we have arrived. He must be taken quietly."

"Agreed," Hawkeye said, his voice echoing their unhappiness. None of them liked to kill from stealth like Meghana and his brethren, but they didn't have a choice this time. The renegades were a blight on the land and there was no choice but to destroy them by any means possible.

The guard's location was a good spot, one that viewed the land around him with a wide vista. But the man was obviously paying more attention to his pipe than he was the surrounding area. All three men crept to the east, moving around him and slowly approaching his position as he blew smoke into the air. Their passage was silent, each step taken with care so that even a deer or rabbit would not hear them had they approached such animals.

It was Uncas whose position was best, who leapt on the man from behind, a hand across the Huron warrior's mouth to prevent his crying out. His knife stabbed upwards against the man twice and he held the warrior on the ground as he struggled and finally fell limp, gasping his last breath. The young Mohican warrior looked saddened for a moment by the death, but cleaned his knife without a word. He picked up the man's musket, knowing an extra weapon could be useful in the coming battle. Chingachgook patted his son's shoulder, understanding the younger man's feelings all too well. Though a veteran of countless battles, the Mohican war chief never took the death of another man as an act to be enjoyed or forgotten. But the death was necessary.

Uncas, for his part, gave his father and adopted brother a brief smile of understanding and soon fell into step behind them as they moved closer to the camp of the raiders. Surprisingly that was the only guard they observed as they slowly moved closer, following the faint traces left behind by men like the guard and Meghana. Few men could find these tracks, but little tell-tale clues were as good as footprints in the mud to Chingachgook, Hawkeye and Uncas. Realizing the Mohawks might have difficulty following them to the cave, which all three could tell was very close based on the smell of cooking smoke over the next ridge, Hawkeye left a pile of rocks directing them towards the raiders' camp.

They climbed for half an hour, moving as silently as they had when approaching the guard. Slowly they began to hear voices, some raised in anger, as they moved closer. All three warriors climbed to the top of the ridge, suddenly having a clear view of the cave that lay beneath. The raiders sat in groups around a cooking fire, a cave directly behind them and a cooking fire near the mouth of the cave. Two men stood facing each other, both snarling with anger though their words were incomprehensible at the distance. But they could see one figure was Meghana and the other was a tall, thin man in buckskins with a dark, thick beard. He was the only white man present and had a long curved sword at his side.

The voices continued to rise, with Meghana pointing his finger at the French Captain and gesticulating wildly. The French officer was replying with equal, if more controlled anger, his gestures indicating that he disliked whatever Meghana was demanding.

Then it happened—a surprise to everyone in the camp as well as the trio looking down from above the cave. Meghana turned away, looking disgusted, and the French officer Dutourd turned towards the cave, his body taut with anger. Just as his back was turned, Meghana spun and struck him hard in the back of his head with his wicked-looking war club. The Frenchman fell hard to the ground and, with a whoop of triumph, Meghana struck the back of the man's head two more times and roared with glee.

The raiders jumped to their feet, some snarling with anger, others obviously taking the side of Meghana. One of the renegades approached Meghana with open anger: a powerful looking Huron warrior with several scars across his face and chest. He stepped close to Meghana and suddenly was forced to leap back as the Mohawk swung at him with his nasty war club. One of Meghana's supporters struck the Huron warrior from behind, hitting the man with the butt-end of an ancient-looking musket. The Huron was sent sprawling, but leapt to his feet with a cry of rage and charged the attacker, slashing out with a wicked-looking dagger.

The raiders began to brawl, twenty men pulling their hand weapons and striking out at those who supported the opposing side in this conflict. These men were all lovers of battle, those who sought to step over their fellow man to get what they wanted rather than working or living in harmony with a tribe. Resentments formed easily, but they'd held those feelings back because the Frenchman had continued to promise them more goods for following his decisions. With the French officer dead, those ill feelings rose and the renegades became a loose band of killers rioting and trying to kill those they disliked.

Meanwhile Meghana was backing away from the fight, knowing he should wait and kill any survivors who didn't agree with his leadership. Dutourd had not been strong enough, preferring to slowly plan the next attack rather than following his lead. Meghana's plan had been simple: circle behind the coming war party and attack the Mohawk encampment. Dutourd considered the plan foolish, stating it did not fit his plans to sow destruction among the English. Meghana understood the French officer's reasoning, but he desired the blood of his former tribe, especially the traitor Yed!

"He is trying to escape." Uncas pointed towards Meghana, who was backing away from the vicious brawl.

"I will go after him," Hawkeye said, beginning to rise but surprised by Chingachgook's restraining hand.

Chingachgook shook his head, “No my soon. If this coward sees you or me, he will flee and hide. Uncas must face him. He will underestimate your younger brother.”

Uncas nodded and smiled, handing his brother his rifle. He reached for his hatchet when his father shook his head and handed him the well-used war club that was always on the elder Mohican’s back. “Father?”

Chingachgook clapped his son on his shoulder, “Take it for this battle, my son. This war club was made by my great-grandfather and used when he fought in battle against many enemies. It will serve you well in this duel of honor.”

Uncas accepted the club, unable to speak, but nodded his thanks. A moment later he was gone and Hawkeye and Chingachgook quickly began loading the rifles and the musket seized earlier from the Huron scout.

“If Meghana ran, we could have tracked him down or shot him. You wanted Uncas to face the man in battle,” Hawkeye observed, sliding forward on the ridge. He knew they needed to protect Uncas from any attacker attempting to help Meghana against his adopted brother.

“I did,” the elder Mohican replied. “He has never dueled a man before. Also if he kills this dog, the Mohawk he favors will look at him with even greater respect and liking. And Meghana is a man who needs to die. Prepare yourself, my son. Your brother is about to reveal himself to the coward.”

Hawkeye smiled at his adopted father’s wisdom but watched as his brother stepped from the clearing. Hawkeye had fought several duels in his short life. A white man among the Mohicans attracted enmity from some, but he’d won each contest. He hadn’t liked to duel other men, but at times in battle there was no other choice. This was Uncas’s chance to understand that part of the path of the warrior.

“Meghana!” Uncas roared, stepping into the open and approaching the twisted-faced man. “Face me, coward!”

Meghana smiled—a horrible sight—at the young Mohican. This one was not his terrifying father or his clever white brother. No, this young pup had probably never killed a man in battle. He would kill this one and then use the remaining survivors to murder the Mohican and the white man as well. Then they would kill the Mohawk and more... It was a glorious thought.

With a cry meant to fill his enemy with fear, Meghana ran forward, swinging his wicked war club for Uncas's eyes. Uncas blocked the attack with the ancestor's war club and tried to trip Meghana. The wily Mohawk warrior leapt out the way of Uncas's foot and swung at the young Mohican's legs. Uncas stumbled back but managed to keep his feet.

Just then a raider spotted the duel between Uncas and Meghana. With a cry of anger, he ran to help the latter, screaming a war cry. Hawkeye jumped out into the open from the top of the ridge, firing down at the raider and toppling him with a precision shot. A second, not yet spotting the Mohican and his adopted white son, also ran to assist Meghana, only to be cut down by a shot from Chingachgook.

One of the renegades spotted the pair on the ridge and stopped the remaining brawlers with a loud call. Pointing up above, he reached for a musket, only to be shot dead by Hawkeye. A second raider fell to the musket formerly the property of the dead Huron, Chingachgook killing the man without pausing.

Realizing the pair on the ridge was alone and needing to reload their weapons, the remaining raiders screamed and led a charge up a path toward their position. Hawkeye and Chingachgook quickly reloaded their rifles, with Hawkeye seizing Uncas's a few seconds later and repeating the laborious exercise. Tossing Uncas's now-loaded rifle over his shoulder to his father, Hawkeye scooped up his own long rifle and fired, killing a raider. Chingachgook caught the rifle and in the same motion fired it at another of the remaining warriors. He dropped the weapon and fired his gun, killing a second. Grabbing the musket, he swung it in the face of a third raider, shattering the man's head.

At the mouth of the cave, Meghana was breathing hard, angered that the young Mohican seemed skilled enough to anticipate his every attack. Striking for the eyes, collar bone, legs or stomach all failed and he found himself barely parrying Uncas's attacks. No, he would need to use his last weapon, one that worked every time he was forced to face a skilled warrior of equal of greater strength and skill.

With a scream of rage, Meghana swung an overhand attack at Uncas's head and was unsurprised that the young warrior parried the attack. But instead of stepping away to attack again, Meghana pushed harder against the young warrior, forcing Uncas to move back to prevent getting his skull crushed. With a rictus grin, Meghana then pulled a knife from his belt and stabbed fast for Uncas's stomach. Many warriors fell to this treacherous attack and soon so would the young Mohican!

Up above Hawkeye blocked a hatchet with his rifle and struck down his attacker with the heavy butt end of the weapon. The warrior fell but was replaced by another, who held a war club over his head and ran for the white warrior. Hawkeye stepped aside, pulled his hatchet from his belt and struck down the attacking brave. Meanwhile, just behind Hawkeye, Chingachgook set about his attackers, using the musket they seized earlier. While not as effective as his war club, three attackers lay at his feet, dead or dying from the Mohican war chief's attacks.

Meghana grinned as stabbed out at Uncas's stomach, but that look turned to surprise and fear as the young Mohican caught his enemy's wrist, stopping the attack. They struggled for several seconds and then the blade began to move slowly, inexorably, towards Meghana's chest.

His eyes wide with fear, Meghana dropped the knife before he could be stabbed and stepped back. Uncas, howling the war cry of his people, swung the club at Meghana's head and was unsurprised that his enemy barely parried the attack. Stepping back, the young Mohican spun in place, bringing the war club hard against Meghana's chest, shattering the warrior's war club and causing the Mohawk to gasp with pain. Lifting the club high, Uncas struck down on Meghana's head, killing him instantly. Howling in triumph, the young Mohican lifted his ancestor's war club high above his head in respect to the warriors of his people.

The remaining raiders, unwilling to face the Mohican war chief and his adopted son, fled rather than meet these two warriors in battle. Eight men lay upon the ground, dead or dying, and Hawkeye slumped to the ground, exhausted.

"Your brother killed his enemy. This was a bloody day, but a good one. Reload your rifle, my son. There are still some dogs who have fled and they will bite if they see us again." Chingachgook smiled down at the younger man. As always he seemed unconcerned by the exhausting battle, a powerful figure who never seemed to tire.

Hawkeye stood weakly but began to load his and Uncas's rifles. Until their Mohawk allies arrived, these hills still possessed dangers. But he sensed the day would be theirs and soon they could help the people of New Hope regain their lives. A difficult few days, but the lands they protected were a little safer now.

Fort of Skulls

I. A. Watson

The wagon was stuck in the ford, one wheel shattered at the axel, and the floodwaters were rising. Half a dozen red-coated British soldiers struggled to drag the cart from the swelling waters. A young lieutenant tugged the carthorses forward to try and get the vehicle moving before it was swept away by the swelling torrent.

"Do we help them?" Uncas asked his father.

Chingachgook stroked a finger across his cheek and considered before he spoke. "The water is rising. If we do not cross now it may be two, three days before the ford is passable again. We will not be back on the Hudson before the new moon."

"If we go down there they'll expect us to drag that wagon out of the river with them," Hawkeye warned. The rain was already coming down hard. He didn't really need to be any wetter.

"We have chosen to ally ourselves with the British," Chingachgook reminded his older son. "That is why we traveled so far to bring General Webb's messages to the fleet at Rockport. Let us offer assistance."

That decided, the three travelers prodded their horses down the muddy slope towards the last feasible crossing point on the swollen Miscatonic. The lieutenant spotted their descent and shouted something to his commander. A moment later the soldiers had abandoned their struggles with the cart and retrieved their rifles.

Chingachgook rode in first, his hands obviously clutching the reins of his spirited paint rather than reaching for his firearms or war-club. He halted in the shallows downstream of the ford and waited to be approached.

The soldiers' captain splashed his own mount flanks-deep through the chilly water and came up to the Indians cautiously. He looked more suspiciously at Hawkeye's fairer skin, then returned his attention to Chingachgook. "What do you want?"

"We intend to cross the river," the experienced tracker replied, indicating himself and his two sons. "Soon the level will be too high."

"You're from round here? You know this territory?"

"We are Mohicans," Uncas said proudly, amazed that the stupid English captain couldn't see that at once. "Our range is far to the west."

"We're carrying messages for your General at Albany," Hawkeye added. "We got papers."

The captain held out his hand to inspect the travel documents. Chingachgook opened the scrip at his waist and handed over the letter of recommendation from the camp courier at Albany and another from his counterparts in Rockport and Gloucester. "These seem to be in order," the officer admitted at last, "but since you're army scouts we'll need your assistance to get to where we're going."

"We're not army scouts," Hawkeye insisted. "We just hired on for a courier job, is all."

"Then you're working for us, far as I'm concerned," the captain insisted. "We need pathfinders to get us to Fort Woburn, south and west of here."

"What happened to your last guide?"

The captain scowled. "Ran off in the night. Don't know why. I was told he was reliable."

Chingachgook exchanged glances with his sons. "We will take you to your fort," he agreed. The route was much the same as they would have followed anyway.

"You know the place?" This question came from the young lieutenant who'd ridden up to support his captain. The youngster's uniform was new, Hawkeye noted.

"We can find it," Uncas promised. Forts were usually easy to locate, either by the smoke of their cooking fires or the noise of their industry.

"Before he ran off, our guide said we'd be there tomorrow," the captain reported.

Hawkeye dropped from his horse. "You won't be there at all if you let the floodwaters wash away your supplies. Come on, Uncas. Let's get that cart across the water."

Uncas followed his adoptive brother to where the soldiers waited warily. Hawkeye inspected the broken wheel and proclaimed the axel good. "It's just broken a pin and a couple of spars is all," he judged. "If we lift the side up we can get the wheel back on and jam a nail in there to pin it on for now. Enough to walk it to the shore anyhow."

An Irish sergeant chivvied the men into action. "Y' heard the man! Potter, Scargill, McCrothy, Broome, take the weight. Clitheroe, lad, you lift the wheel back onto the shaft. Put y' backs into it!"

Hawkeye and Uncas lent a hand to raise the laden cart so the wheel could be repinned to the axel. By the time the job was done the floodwaters were almost topping the boards of the wagon. Chingachgook coaxed the exhausted shivering horses to a last labor and the cart was hauled onto the muddy bank. The water was up to the soldiers' waists as they pressed across the flooded ford.

The final member of the soldiers' party, a shriveled ancient Chinaman, scurried forward to take charge of the wagon once again. His wrinkled face was bruised where he'd been hit for catching the cartwheel in a river rut in the first place.

When the cart had ground its way up onto dry ground on the southern bank Hawkeye retrieved his Kentucky long rifle from his father and replaced his powder horn at his belt.

One of the soldiers spat a wad of tobacco and eyed the weapon. "That's a good gun," the man they called Potter said. The British issued their redcoats with crude Brown Bessies, inaccurate beyond sixty yards. "Know how to use it?"

"I can shoot," answered Hawkeye. He didn't like the trooper's tone.

Potter considered that for a moment. "I killed me dozens of Indians," he said at last.

Uncas took a step forward to make an angry retort. Chingachgook laid a restraining hand on his shoulder. "Do not respond to the words of fools," he advised his son in their native tongue.

The young lieutenant rode up, wringing out the tails of his smart uniform coat. "Good work," he approved. "May I know your names?"

"I am Chingachgook, the Great Serpent, a chief of the Mohicans. White men sometimes call me John Mohegan. This is my white son Hawkeye the Deerslayer, La Longue Carabine, and this Uncas, my son by Wah-ta-Wah. He is the last pure-blood of my people."

"I'm James Eckland, of Exeter, England," the lieutenant responded. "I'm new to the colonies, with the Third Devonshire Rifles. That's Captain Peabody. The sergeant's called Rourke."

"You're all heading out to reinforce Fort Woburn?" Uncas guessed.

"Yes. We're to replace losses they took from French snipers. Woburn's a new fort, built less than a year ago. It's not cleaned out the nearby territory yet."

The soldiers took some time to make better repairs on their cart. That meant unshipping the supplies that ladened it. The Mohicans watched as barrels of salted pork and lard and ale were lifted to the turf. Then came a crate of firearms, two sealed barrels of black powder, a half dozen boxes of sundry kitchen materials, and a metal strongbox carrying the garrison's payroll.

"Don't get any ideas," Sergeant Rourke warned the scouts.

"We're not thieves," Hawkeye told him. He wondered whether the guide that had run away had been similarly insulted.

At least one of the soldiers had some delicacy. "No offence meant," Trooper Broome told them. ""We just don't want no misunderstandings."

"I think we understand," Chingachgook answered.

"We're a bit on edge, is all," Broome explained. "It's this journey, 'cross this country. The landscape's so bleak and morbid. The rain never stops but otherwise everything's so quiet. We've been getting more and more edgy ever since we marched out of Ipswich."

Hawkeye had to make some allowance for that. There was something about these lonely marshlands that troubled the young scout. The Miscatonic Valley's sparse stands of wood and stubbly undulating plains were different from the thick green forests of his home, but it was more than that. The trees seemed mean and twisted, crouched against the sea-winds like wicked old men. The louring sky over the lonely tumuli that dotted the landscape seemed to threaten evil.

"We'll get you to your fort as soon as possible," Hawkeye promised Broome. "And then we'll be on our way."

"I do not like this place," admitted Uncas. It was the next morning but the rain had not let up. The persistent drizzle made the ground spongy. The carthorses' hooves slipped often and the soldiers were foul-tempered and mud splattered. The land had risen steadily and now the forest was more dense but no friendlier. "I do not like the tall mounds of stone that stand like sentinels on the high places."

Chingachgook knew something of their mystery. "This was the range of the Misqas before the white man came. They were a strange people, even to the Algonquin. It was they who tended the old cairns and strange pyramids, but whether they built them I do not know. They worshipped snakes and lizards and spirits under the ground and in the stars."

"Their land feels sick," Hawkeye judged. "I felt it at Gloucester, but worse here. Is it because the Misqas were all killed that their land mourns?"

"I dreamed of the Misqas last night," Chingachgook confessed. "They were all pale like the white man, with hair bleached as elders, and no color in their eyes. They did not seem to welcome me."

Hawkeye was more disturbed by his father's dream than the threat of French snipers or the rumors that an Abenaki war party might roam the land. "What did the spirits want?"

"I do not know. I was woken by the cry of the whip-poor-whil." The Mohican chief shrugged. "It was a night vision. Looking at it in daylight will only make it vanish."

Hawkeye veered off to the left and found a tiny culvert stream cutting through the sedge-grass. He gestured Uncas and Chingachgook over. "Someone was here."

The scouts examined the marks. "Soft-slippered," Uncas noted. That meant a tribesman, not a white settler. "Broad-footed. A man."

"A day ago, no more," Chingachgook added. He scooped a fingerful of rain-soaked mud from the print and smelled it.

"Heading north," Hawkeye observed. "Away from our destination."

The sound of horses indicated that the main party had caught up with the scouts. Captain Peabody rode over to see what the guides were huddled over. Hawkeye demonstrated the footprint.

"Not our concern if they were going away," Peabody decided. "Keep on towards Woburn."

The land dipped again into a shallow basin. The little stream joined with others to form one of the small lakes that dotted the area. Another tumulus marked the edge of the treeline. The valley floor was a weed-tangled maze of gorse thickets.

Hawkeye spotted something at the far edge of the water. "There. Is that a landing?"

Uncas shielded his eyes with his hand and stared. "Yes. And two rowing boats tied to the jetty. Is that Fort Woburn?"

"Tell father we're going down to see."

Captain Peabody called a halt while the scouts rode round the lake to identify whatever buildings might be associated with the landing. Hawkeye and Uncas took their horses down into the maze of bushes and followed the slope to the waters edge.

The grey lake was still and silent. The leatherstockings trotted their mounts around the edge of the pool towards the wooden jetty. They saw a flag above the tall weeds, and then spotted the outer stockade of a wooden fort.

"That's the place," Uncas decided. "But why no smoke? Don't they have cook-fires?"

"No noise either," Hawkeye added. "No hammering, no marching, no animals, nothing." He slipped off his horse. "Tether the horses here. We'll go in quietly."

Uncas followed Hawkeye in single file through the remaining cover, up to the cleared perimeter around the fort. Hawkeye indicated the painted pegs staked around the open area; ranging markers for rifle fire. This was a working fort that took its defense seriously.

Except there was no-one on either watchtower, and no guard walked the stockade wall.

Hawkeye checked that his rifle was in good condition, loaded and primed. He loosened his knife in his belt-sheath. He padded stealthily but quickly over the open ground between the bushes and the heavy gate. Uncas followed five steps behind.

There was still no response. No challenge came from within Fort Woburn. The rain-damped ground showed no recent passage through the wooden entrance.

"What is this?" Uncas breathed. Hawkeye gestured for silence.

He leaned on the gate. It was unbarred. It opened a little at his push.

Hawkeye slipped through the thin gap into the stockade's yard. The layout was the same as a hundred new-made forts across the colonies, an outer perimeter of staked tree-trunks shored with an interior scaffolding to make a high walkway, then a central green edged with huts and storehouses.

Nobody was there.

Uncas slid in behind Hawkeye and looked around, his rifle hefted ready to fire.

Hawkeye indicated that his brother should cover him, then crept along the edge of the compound to the first building – a stable. He lifted the latch and pushed the door ajar. Twenty stalls were well supplied with hay and oats, but there were no horses.

Next round was a smithy. The front wall was a pair of wicker doors, designed so the building could be opened up to let heat and smoke escape from the forge. Those doors were wide apart, pegged in place so the workshop could be used. The fire had died out, leaving flaky grey ash. Leaves had blown into the corners of the room.

Uncas shifted uncomfortably. Hawkeye moved on.

The third hut was a storehouse, padlocked shut. Beyond that was a mess hall, as empty as the rest. The kitchen behind it was stocked with provisions, but the meat on the butcher's table was rancid with lazy maggots.

Hawkeye checked every building. The barracks huts contained the bedrolls and personal effects of the fifty-plus men who'd been stationed here. Some uniforms were hung to dry around a stove. No weapons were present. The commander's cabin was neat and orderly, but deserted. The administration building, the hospital tent, the chapel, all were empty of human life.

"No men, no horses, no dogs, no cats, no cows for milk or chickens for eggs," Hawkeye recounted to Uncas. "Nothing bigger'n an insect living here. Not even rats."

"What happened?" Uncas worried. "How can fifty soldiers just vanish?"

"I don't know. We must return and tell father and Captain Peabody. Night's not far off and it will be better to sleep inside secure walls."

"Even these walls?"

Hawkeye had no answer to that.

The British soldiers were no happier with the discoveries at the fort than were the scouts. "What could make five dozen men disappear like they never existed?" Trooper McCrothy demanded, crossing himself.

"Hold y' tongue!" Sergeant Rourke snapped harshly. "This isn't the time to have vapors like a woman. Nightfall's nearly on us and I want this place secured. Clitheroe, Scargill, stable the horses. Potter, get that gate barred. Woo, get a fire going in that kitchen. Broome, McCrothy, up on the towers, set a watch. Now!"

The soldiers hastened at their sergeant's bark. The old Chinaman scurried away to the kitchens. Captain Peabody and Lieutenant Eckland remained to confer.

"Have you any idea what happened here?" Peabody asked the scouts.

Hawkeye shook his head. "The gate was unbarred. They might all have left, I suppose."

"And abandoned everything?" Peabody scorned. "If they evacuated, retreated for some reason, they'd have taken supplies, bedding, records. They'd have taken the flag."

Chingachgook agreed. "There are parts of the fort that my son did not search," he noted. "We must look in the locked rooms for more clues."

Peabody considered that. "Very well. Eckland, you investigate. Take one of these fellows with you."

"I'll go," Hawkeye offered. "Uncas, you'd better help out with the watch. I'll relieve you later."

"Take station over the gate," Peabody ordered. "Lord knows that a handful of men like us would be sore pressed to defend this fort but it's better than nothing."

Uncas nodded and slipped off into the gathering dusk. Chingachgook allowed Hawkeye to be dragged off with the young lieutenant. It was clear that the older tracker wanted some time to look around alone. Peabody vanished into the interior of the administration house.

"Where shall we look first?" Eckland wondered.

"The storehouse was sealed," Hawkeye remembered.

It wasn't too hard to force the padlock. Hawkeye jimmied the hasp and Eckland cautiously pushed the door open. The interior of the store was dark and quiet. The searchers lit storm lanterns and walked along the aisles between the shelves.

"About half full," Eckland noted. "They didn't run out of provisions in any case."

Hawkeye ran a hand through a split sack of sawbeans and checked a barrel of flour. There were weevils in the hard tack but that wasn't unusual. There was no sign of larger vermin, though.

Eckland tried to refasten the broken lock as best he could. Evidently he didn't trust his men not to plunder the store for liquor.

The next sealed space was the arsenal. The door was sturdier here, so at Hawkeye's suggestion they checked the admin office and found a bunch of keys on a hook beside the clerk's desk. That got them into the small thick-walled hut where barrels of gunpowder were stored. With Eckland's permission, Hawkeye filled a couple of horns and took a handful of shot.

"There's nothing to indicate anything strange happened," the lieutenant puzzled. "This inventory sheet was filled in as normal three days ago, and then – nothing!"

"That gives us a time when the men vanished," Hawkeye suggested. The date was consistent with the spoiled meat and the thin accumulation of dust.

The infirmary tent was filled with leaves. The flap had been left open so the floor was filled with blown debris. Two wooden cots waited, stripped of linen, clearly unused in the days just before the camp had emptied.

The chapel yielded little too, save for a memorial book recording the funerals of each man that had died since the fort's foundation ten months before. A little plot beyond the east wall had been set aside as a graveyard.

In the writing desk at the rear of the church, where the ledger had been stored, Hawkeye found a strange tangle of old bones and soapstone bound together with leather thread. The whole thing sat on the palm of his hand. He had no idea at all what it was. "I'll ask father," he decided and dropped the thing into his pouch.

The next logical building was the cookhouse at the rear of the mess hall. Rourke was present, drinking with Clitheroe and Scargill; Hawkeye wondered if they'd already discovered the busted lock on the stores. The old Chinaman everybody called Woo clattered around roasting meat for a late supper. The smell of the pork was enticing.

While Lieutenant Ekland consulted with the sergeant, Hawkeye took a moment to speak with Woo. "You understand English?" he asked the old man.

Woo turned a spit and nodded.

"I'm Hawkeye of the Mohicans. Natty Poe to white folks."

The old man nodded again. "Wǔ dà láng," he replied.

"That's your name?"

"Wǔ dà láng."

"Is it alright if I call you Wu?"

Another nod.

"You got any idea what the heck's going on here, Wu?" Hawkeye wondered.

A shake of the head. Wu turned the meat again and added a pan of greens onto the stove.

"You any idea why that other guide ran off, maybe?"

Wu looked around to make sure the soldiers were busy chattering with each other. "Red man was scared," the cook confided.

"What of?" Hawkeye asked.

Wu pointed round at Fort Woburn. "This place."

"Why?"

The Chinaman shrugged.

"He didn't say no more?"

Wu gestured to the east, where the jetty jutted into the lake. "Bad waters. That is all."

By now it was fully dark outside. Rourke had torches and lanterns lit to illuminate the compound. The lights seemed insufficient for the task. Dark shadows seeped between the little pools of yellow warmth, pressing in, waiting.

As Hawkeye emerged from the second barracks hut he heard Uncas call a challenge from his watch-place above the main gate. Broome and McCrothy tensed on their watchtowers until Chingachgook called back to identify himself. Hawkeye hadn't known that his father had left the compound.

When the Mohican chief had been readmitted to the fort, Lieutenant Ekland hurried over to hear if he had news. "What did you find out there? Any tracks of our missing men?"

"No tracks," Chingachgook answered. As far as Hawkeye was concerned that meant there were none to find. "Some old signs of ten or eleven Abenaki two weeks ago, probably scouting the fort, but nothing since."

Hawkeye could see something was troubling his father, though. "What else was there?" he asked.

Chingachgook frowned. "We had better talk to Captain Peabody," he suggested.

The dour captain was sat in the naval chair behind the commander's desk, trying to find any clue in Major Bracewood's logs about what might have happened to the missing cohort. He'd checked the supply legers and the daily reports and come to the same conclusions about all routine in the camp stopping abruptly three days ago.

As Ekland entered with Chingachgook and Hawkeye, Peabody laid aside the journal and scowled in frustration. "I hope you found out more than I did," he growled.

"Equipment in good order, plenty of supplies, nothing out of place," the young lieutenant reported, dismayed. "Nothing to say where our men went – or even how!"

"There are no tracks," worried Hawkeye. "That many men and horses would leave an easy trail."

"But they're not here!" Peabody exploded. "If they're not here then they left. Even if they were all slaughtered by the Abenaki there would be corpses, blood on the ground, something."

Hawkeye pointed to a sturdy door at the rear of the commander's office. "We haven't looked in there," he noted.

"It's a strong-room," the captain replied. "We put our pay-chest in there along with the company pay-chest."

Ekland's brows rose. "The men of Fort Woburn deserted without taking the treasury? Surely no door, however strong…"

"It's another mystery," Peabody agreed. "This place is full of them." Without his bluster he looked like a tired old man fighting his last war.

"There is something else," Chingachgook said quietly. His deep voice demanded attention. His demeanor was grave. "I know now why your guide fled, Captain Peabody."

"And why's that?" demanded the officer.

"You have seen the Misqat cairns at the high places and crossroads of this land," Chingachgook noted. "Once all this was their place, from the bay you call Kingsport to far in the north. When white settlers came there was battle and disease and now the Misqat are no more."

"What's that got to do with our missing soldiers?" Ekland demanded.

Chingachgook would not be hurried. “I have found Misqat stones near this fort. They have all been broken - pushed over and scattered.”

A shiver ran through Hawkeye. “Why? By who?”

His father pointed from Peabody to Ekland. “By your people, I believe. There were signs of ropes and chains and horses to drag down the cairns. Quite recently, I think.”

“What for?” puzzled Ekland. “That makes no sense.”

Peabody flicked back in the pages of Major Bracewood’s journal. “It might make some sense of entries in this log where the fort commander wrote that men had been sent out on land clearing duties. As to why…?”

“I know what the cairns were now, too,” Chingachgook reported. “There were bones beneath the stones. They were very old, almost gone to dust. I do not recognize the animals. I do not believe they were human – at least not men like us. Only fragments remain. They have been raked away with the stones.”

“This whole area is a burial ground,” Hawkeye realized. “Wu said the waters were bad. This is a place of death.”

Lieutenant Ekland shifted uneasily. “I don’t understand,” he admitted, “You’re saying this fort is built on a graveyard?”

Hawkeye remembered the object in his pouch and passed it to his father. “This was in the church, in a drawer. It has soil on it. I think maybe they dug it up when they were burying bodies in that plot outside the stockade.”

Chingachgook examined the object. “I do not know this thing,” he admitted. He returned it to his son.

Captain Peabody slammed the ledger shut with sudden temper. “This is ridiculous! Indian graveyards and vanished garrisons! I won’t have it! I will not!” He jabbed a finger at Ekland. “You, sir, will see that there’s a good watch kept tonight in case the Abenaki return for more ‘scouting’. And you two, there will be no loose talk of dead Indians and weird cairns, do you understand. Spook my soldiers and I'll have you flogged!"

Hawkeye bristled. Chingachgook nodded.

Peabody hadn't finished. "Tomorrow one of you will ride courier to Ipswich with word of what's happened here. We need urgent reinforcements before the French work out we couldn't stand against an attack for more then ten minutes."

"Hold on," objected Hawkeye. "We're headed for the Hudson. We already have letters to carry. We can't turn back to the coast again, even if we could cross the flooded Miscatonic."

"I didn't say you'd all go," Peabody warned. He pointed to Chingachgook. "You'll go. Your sons will stay here, with us, to make sure you take the message and bring rescue back. That way you won't disappear like our last guide."

Chingachgook's face darkened. "You threaten my sons to compel my aid?"

Hawkeye's temper flared too. "We helped you! We dragged your sorry cart out of the river mud and got you to your fort. This is how you repay us?"

"I do what I have to!" Captain Peabody shouted. "Right now I've got eight soldiers to hold a fort and a territory that Major Bracewood struggled to hold with fifty. If the French come south they could punch a gap in our defenses and be on Kingsport and Marblehead before anyone knows it. That will not happen on my watch. So get the idea into your heads that word'll be taken to Ipswich and Gloucester, or else I'll be stringing Indians up as a warning to all turncoats everywhere not to argue with His Majesty's army!"

Chingachgook stared into the British officer's eyes. "You have stumbled onto an ancient horror here, white man. Your missing Major foolishly disturbed the mounds. Whatever that awoke, it is likely still out there, beyond your walls. Maybe even inside your walls. A wise leader would take his men and flee."

"A coward might. I'm an Englishman!"

"You are a fool. You will stay here, where something was able to spirit away five times the number of soldiers you have, take them with little sign of their passing, and you will wait for the same thing to happen to you. And you intend to hold my sons here and risk their lives too."

Lieutenant Ekland tried to intervene between the angry men. "There's no point in shouting with respect. The situation here has got us all a little disturbed. But Mister Mohigan, surely you can see that we can't just abandon our post? We have a duty to hold this fort, even at the cost of our lives. And if there is danger here then help must be summoned. You are our best, perhaps our only chance of doing that."

"Compelling us to help isn't the way!"" Hawkeye warned.

"I won't beg from damned red-skins!" Peabody blustered.

"Then you are an even bigger fool," Chingachgook replied. "I would beg for my sons. Die for them. But since you are such a fool I will take your message. Hawkeye and Uncas will stay here to protect your men from your foolishness as best they can, and I will report your folly to your superiors."

There were more bitter words exchanged, but the end result was the same. Just before first light the Mohican chief parted from his sons and vanished into the mist-swathed forest.

The outcry came at dawn, as Mr. Wu went to bank up the cookhouse fire in preparation for the soldiers' breakfast. His panicked shrieks alerted the watch. Hawkeye had relieved Uncas in the middle of the night, so it was he who gestured for Broome to stay on lookout at his tower post and dropped down to the courtyard after McCrothy.

The Chinaman had rushed out of the kitchen and now stood nervously on the muddy parade ground. Clitheroe and Potter had been getting up to relieve the watch and were first at the scene. Sergeant Rourke arrived at the same time as Hawkeye made it across the compound.

"Alright, what's this?" Rourke demanded, shouldering Potter aside and fixing his stare on Wu.

Hawkeye ignored the frightened cook and went into the kitchen. A pile of logs for the fire was spilled across the floor where Woo had dropped them. A barrel of jerked beef was open on the crude plank trestle.

A man's skull sat atop the pile of dried meat.

Hawkeye suppressed the superstitious pang that chilled him through. He advanced into the cookhouse, looking round. He only realized later that his hand had pulled his knife.

His eyes were drawn again to the white polished skull atop the provisions box. It grinned back at him, its empty sockets revealing nothing about how it had come to be there or how it had appeared in a locked hut in a guarded fort.

Rourke, Clitheroe, and Potter pressed into the kitchen. Potter dragged Wu by his pigtails and tossed the Chinaman brutally to the floor. "You'll tell us what you did, you yellow heathen, or by God I'll flay skin off your back," the brutal soldier promised.

Uncas slipped quietly through the door and exchanged a look with his brother.

"There is no point talking to Mr. Wu until he calms down," Hawkeye suggested. "But there are other things to check. Someone sneaked in here by night to put the skull here. That means that someone of the fort's company did this thing or else someone breached the walls. We need to search the place again, but more carefully this time, checking all the places an enemy might hide."

"Where did the skull come from?" Uncas asked. "It's fresh."

"Fresh? What'd'you mean fresh?" Rourke demanded.

Hawkeye forced himself to pick up the unexpected intruder and handle it. "The bone is not decayed or discolored. This has never been buried in soil. It is cleaned off and polished, as one might preserve a trophy kill. It was probably boiled."

"Is that a man's skull?" Potter asked in horror, "Or an Indian's?"

Hawkeye ignored the soldier. "Uncas, we saw a cemetery outside the wall. Check if any graves have been disturbed."

Uncas stiffened a moment at the idea of going alone to a burial ground when the dead appeared to be leaving parts of themselves nearby, but he nodded and slipped away as quietly as he'd come.

"You said that skull had never been buried," Rourke objected.

"It never lay in the soil," Hawkeye replied. "It might have lain in a coffin. Best to check."

"It's an omen," McCrothy declared in a quiet, frightened voice. "It's a sign that whatever claimed all the soldiers who were here before is coming to take us too!"

"Belay that!" shouted Rourke, right in the soldier's face. "I'll have none o' your sniveling cowardly jabberings here, McCrothy. I've got my eye on you!"

Hawkeye checked the cookhouse. The shutters were still down, bolted from the inside. The door had been locked; Woo had dropped the big iron key taken from the administration office bunch. There were no other obvious ways of entry.

"Who locked up?" Hawkeye asked.

"I did," said Rourke. "And the keys went back to Captain Peabody."

Hawkeye knelt down beside the Chinaman. Wu was trembling less down but one eye was swelling where Potter had hit him? "Did you get the key from the Captain this morning, Mr. Wu?"

The cook nodded.

Potter spat. "He could'a set this whole thing up. He couldn't sneaked that skull in and set up all that fuss to fright us!"

"And where did he get the skull?" Hawkeye asked scornfully.

"Who knows what those Heathens carry in their kit?"

Hawkeye turned his back on Potter and helped Wu to his feet. "Carry on making breakfast," the tracker advised. "We'll report to Captain Peabody."

"But don't use that jerky!" McCrothy pleaded. "If it's not poisoned then it's cursed!"

"We need to tell the Captain," Sergeant Rourke agreed. "And we need to search."

The first thing the search found was that a man was missing: Scargill was gone.

"He was there at mid-watch!" young Clitheroe swore. "When I used the pot he was snoring away in his bunk."

"Could he have deserted?" Lieutenant Ekland wondered.

"He didn't take his kit with him," Rourke reported. "Not even his musket." The implication was that only a madman would head into the wilderness unarmed.

"Was... was that his skull?" asked McCrothy timidly before his sergeant bellowed him to silence.

"The bones could not have been boiled and cleaned so quickly," Hawkeye judged. Not by human agency, anyway.

Uncas joined the knot of worried men in the admin cabin. "No signs of disturbance amongst the graves," he reported back. "But there was this." He handed Hawkeye a sacking-wrapped bundle. Even before peeling away the burlap Hawkeye knew it was another skull.

Sergeant Rourke swore. Potter pointed an accusing finger at Uncas. "It's them! These redskins! The old one didn't like that we're holding his boys, see, and he's out there sneaking around and murdering us one by one!"

"If Chingachgook wanted you dead he would look you in the eye and end your life!" Uncas declared hotly.

"There's no point making accusations," Hawkeye insisted. "We need to search the fort, carefully, properly. But this time we're not hunting clues to missing troopers. We're looking for a live intruder who may move around to evade us."

The scout made sense. Peabody nodded. "What do you suggest?"

Hawkeye thought quickly. "Two men watching from the towers. Two more to guard whichever building we are searching, so nobody can escape. Another in the courtyard to prevent anyone from entering buildings we have already inspected. The rest of us checking each hut in close detail."

The Captain nodded. "Ekland, make it happen."

The hunt began.

The hunt ended. "It makes no account," argued Sgt Rourke, spooked by the complete absence of clues about Scargill's disappearance. "If he was murdered, where's his body? If he ran, how did he get out of a sealed fort? It can't happen!"

"But it did," Lt. Ekland argued. He tried to keep his voice calm, gentlemanly, like they'd trained him to at Woolwich. He failed.

Uncas still knelt on the bunkhouse floor, riffling through the straw matting as if hoping that the missing soldier would somehow be hidden there. The last pureblood Mohican was also disquieted. “There must be some secret we have not yet found, brother,” he insisted.

Hawkeye had led the search through each of the fort’s buildings as he’d proposed: stable, smithy, stores, barracks huts, mess, commander's cabin, admin building, hospital tent, arsenal, chapel. He thought hard about what he’d seen.

“The smithy wicker was open,” he considered. “The pest tent’s flap was tied back. That means it was daytime when the other soldiers vanished. They took horses, but left behind what supplies and arms they couldn’t carry.”

“And their personal belongings,” Uncas pointed out. “Why abandon those?”

Hawkeye didn’t know. “The stable’s not that big. There can’t have been more than a dozen horses here. There are tracks of them coming and going all over the place, but no way to know which was their final departure. Or, I suppose, whether the horses were taken away by whoever got the troopers here.”

“I’m less interested in where those other fellows went than what became of Dan Scargill,” Rourke admitted. “How can a man just vanish from his bunk?”

Hawkeye thought that a better question might be why. “Did Scargill like his liquor?” he asked.

“As much as the next man and better‘n most,” the sergeant reported. His mind caught up with the leatherstocking’s. “You’re thinking that maybe he crept out by night knowing that the supply hut wasn’t secured, hoping for a jug of the good stuff?”

“Is that likely, Rourke?” asked Lt. Eckland.

“He was a sneaky little bastard, begging y’ pardon for my French. One o’ the lads must have gotten the bottles I took off’a them last night, and I’d finger Scargill or Potter before the rest of ‘em. So, yeah, he might have decided to wait till it was quiet and go back for some more.”

"We should look in the storehouse again," Uncas urged.

The other redcoats were still keeping watch-stations on the fort buildings. Ekland led Rourke and the Indians back to the long supplies shed. He unpicked the thick twisted wire that sealed the broken front door lock and slipped inside.

And stopped short.

There, laid in the middle of the aisle that they'd searched not an hour before, was a third polished skull.

"Mother of God!" breathed Rourke, crossing himself.

Hawkeye took a step across the threshold. Uncas caught him. "Don't go in there, brother. It is a cursed place!"

The deerhunter shook him off. "We cannot fear the dead. They outnumber us too much." He padded into the shadowed store-hut, long knife in hand.

Ekland called to the sentry in the centre of the yard. "Broome! Has anyone been near this shed?"

"No sir, not that I saw. Not since you searched it before."

"Then how…?" breathed Rourke.

Hawkeye crawled over the floor, examining it carefully. He found no blood, no mark to suggest that Scargill had ever been here. He tried the back door and found it securely locked. He opened every crate and barrel to see that nothing ill lurked inside. He discovered nothing to show how a polished skull might materialize in a deserted hut. Except…

"When we came to search this hut earlier, was the wire sealing it shut twisted the way you left it?" he asked Ekland.

The young lieutenant tried to remember. "Not sure. I didn't pay attention. Why?"

"Because if the soldier Scargill did creep in here to steal, then either he or some other closed up the door afterwards to hide his crime."

"If Scargill was taken in here then it could not be he who sealed the store," Uncas considered.

"Taken in here?" Rourke objected. "Taken where? By who?"

"If he was murdered here then his murderer retwisted the wire," Hawkeye reasoned. "But he might as well have been attacked as he slipped through the darkness between the huts."

"We should check again for traces there," Uncas suggested.

Another thought occurred to Hawkeye. He pointed at the keyring that Ekland carried. "Those keys we found in the administration office. How many are there?"

"Five," the lieutenant replied. "Why?"

"The key for Captain Peabody's office and for the strongroom behind it were never on here. You gave Wu the keys to the mess hall and kitchen larder. There is the arsenal key and the small one for the holy wine store in the chapel. That one is for the big medicine cupboard in the hospital tent. That, I think, for the powder store locker. This last one must be for the broken lock on this storeroom. So where is the key for the back door?"

Ekland looked at the ring in his hand. He checked each key one by one. He tried them all at the sealed rear entrance. There was no match for the unbroken lock of the storage hut.

"That makes no sense," he frowned.

"If someone had the key, he could have slipped in back to plant that skull and Broome wouldn't see him," Hawkeye suggested.

"I need to report all this to Captain Peabody. You Indians, go on the walls and join the watch. Rourke, put that skull with the other two."

The sergeant opened his mouth to protest, "Me, sir?" but his discipline held at the last. He lifted the polished cranium with obvious dread and hurried to deposit it in the commander's office with the others.

"Three hours until darkness," Uncas said to Hawkeye.

Apart from Clitheroe with Ekland on the walls, the rest of the common soldiers gathered together at sunset in the mess for wait for orders from Captain Peabody. Only good discipline and proper co-ordination would prevent morale from crumbling now.

"We should flee this godforsaken place," superstitious McCrothy muttered to his fellows as they huddled over the mince and chickpeas served up by Wu. "We should run back to Ipswich. Let the damn Froggies have this fort. Let them do the dying here."

"Don't be soft," growled Potter. "It's them greasy redskins and their witchcraft. Give me ten minutes with 'em and a hot knife and we'd find out what they did with Scargill soon enough."

"Hawkeye and Uncas weren't here when Major Bracewood and all the rest vanished," Broome pointed out.

"How d'you know that?" Potter persisted. "They could'a killed our boys here, tortured out of 'em that reinforcements was coming, then set off to bring us to our deaths too. That old man of theirs might have ridden off to bring his whole stinking tribe back to massacre us!"

"It's this land," McCrothy insisted. "There's something twisted and wrong about it. That lake's too still. No ripples. And those damned birds making their evil calls all night. They say they only fall silent when a man dies, while they're devouring his soul!"

"Shut up!" Sgt. Rourke ordered his men. "Wild talk won't do nothing to keep us alive. I'm not saying don't keep an eye out on the redskins and the Chinaman – but keep the other on the horizon. And keep y' lips buttoned."

"You've heard the stories too, though, sarge," McCrothy whispered. "You must have, back in Ipswich. Strange lights under the sea at Dunwich point. That siren they saw on the Manuxet River by the Inns-mouth. That island in the

Miscatonic with the sacrifice stone. Those dug-up graves on Hangman's Hill. This whole area's the devil's playground, and we'll not be safe till we're a hundred miles away!"

Rourke clenched his fist. "I said shut it! This is no time for talk like that. Just shut it!"

Across the too-large mess hall, Uncas and Hawkeye ate separately. They had not been offered food from the soldier's common pot. Disdaining the hard-tack set aside for them they ate from their pouches, finishing the last of a rabbit that Chingachgook had taken down yesterday.

Uncas glanced over at the huddle of redcoats. "They will turn on us," he predicted. "They are frightened, and fools."

"We better be careful," Hawkeye agreed, "but remember that father placed them under our care. We gotta do what we can to preserve them." He fingered the odd soapstone with its disquieting edges. "Something terrible happened to the men of this fort. I'm feared that it's happening again."

"What can we do against the magic of a dead race?" Uncas worried.

Before Hawkeye could formulate an answer, Ekland hurried into the mess. Expecting their commanding officer to be right behind the new lieutenant, the soldiers assembled in a straggling parade line.

Ekland was as pale as a corpse and trembling. "The Major..." he reported like a man pronouncing sentence of death. "He was in his office, writing the log. Writing..."

The youngster nearly fell. Hawkeye hurried over to hold him up. "What else?" he demanded, for surely a mere disappearance was not enough to send the junior officer to the edge of distraction. "Wu, find spirits. Mr. Broome, go with him. Uncas, Sgt Rourke, come with me. The rest of you, look to the lieutenant."

"Who put you in charge, halfbreed?" Potter sneered. "I say..."

"Shut the hell up and do as you're told," Rourke snapped at the private. "Hawkeye, lead the way, son."

The longstockings checked their rifles and hastened out of the lamp-lit mess into the darkness. "Get on the wall," Hawkeye thought to tell Uncas. "The boy Clitheroe's alone there. This might be a distraction."

Uncas nodded and ghosted into the night.

"You think fast on y' feet, scout," Rourke admired. He trailed behind Hawkeye as they hastened to the admin cabin.

Ekland had left the front door wide open. The outer office was shadowed, lit by a single storm lantern that merely revealed the outline of two desks, a bureau, some filing cupboards. Hawkeye entered cautiously, ranging his Kentucky long-rifle left and right before passing on to the fort commander's sanctum.

He eased open the inner door with his moccasin. A three-branch candelabrum on Major Bracewood's desk illuminated the scene that had sent Ekland fleeing.

A man sat in the commander's place; or at least what had once been a man. A pulped, skinned half-skeleton now reclined in the naval chair. Great chunks of flesh had been torn from his limbs, but he still wore the tatters of a redcoat uniform.

Rourke swore. "What… what on God's clean Earth could possibly have done that to Captain Peabody?"

Hawkeye gestured him to silence. He stared round the small chamber, trying to see if anything else was out of place. The window was shuttered and sealed. The strongroom at the rear was still locked off. The tallow candles were half-burned down, as they might have been had Peabody lit them when twilight fell.

There was a quill pen in the dead man's fist. It was poised over the log-book where the Captain had been recording the circumstances of the abandoned fort.

Rourke vomited on the doorstep.

Hawkeye examined the flayed corpse. "This ain't Captain Peabody."

"What? What d'you mean?"

"It is not the Captain. See the weave of his uniform? Cruder, poorer. A common soldier's thread." The face was gone but there were other signs. "See the teeth? Stained with tobacco and rotted. This was a common man." Hawkeye hesitated. "I think this was Scargill."

"Scargill? But how?"

The tracker prodded his knife into the cadaver's remaining fleshy parts. "This man died less'n a day ago. He's not rotted. His organs are still soft. But no blood in him. He was drained of it, like a hung pig."

Rourke clung to the lintel and looked sickly at his former soldier. He tried to find a question to formulate but his lips couldn't find the words.

Hawkeye pointed to sharp scraped grooves on the long bones of Scargill's arms. "These are like the marks a butcher leaves on a cow or horse when he carves it for meat."

Ekland was calmer when Hawkeye and Rourke returned to the hall. Wu had got most of a bottle of whisky into the officer and the youngster was half-way to dozing. Potter, McCrothy, and Broome were skulking in a corner, muttering to each other, but they rushed over as their sergeant appeared.

"Is it true?" they demanded. "Peabody gutted in his own chair?"

"Not the Captain, lads," Rourke had to tell them. "Dan Scargill. We've no idea where our commander is."

"I have," said Hawkeye.

"You got anything to confess, half-breed, you better spit it our now!" warned Potter.

"Don't be a damnfool," the guide snapped back. The bigot's constant accusations were wearing thin. "I been thinking on how someone might have gotten into this camp and done the stuff that's been happening. Now they might get over the wall with such a light watch, but not during daytime. And we searched nearly everywhere."

"Nearly?" Broome caught the qualification. "Where didn't we look?"

"There's that strong-room at back of the commander's office. The one with the pay boxes in. Captain Peabody said it was empty, but it's the only place we've not searched ourselves."

Potter and McCrothy exchanged looks. "Two pay chests…" Potter breathed.

"Don't be getting any ideas, soldier," Sergeant Rourke warned.

"But all that coin, Sarge," McCrothy argued. "Think about it. Why stay here to get chopped up by ghosts? We could take that treasury, split it between us, and make a run for… Salem, maybe, or Marblehead. Not Kingsport, because there'd be too many troops there. We could slip down the coast to Boston, take ship…"

"Shut your mouth, McCrothy, afore I shut it for you! You're in the king's service, damn it, and I won't have you disgrace yourself and y' regiment!"

The superstitious Irishman might have argued more, but Potter laid a restraining hand on his sleeve. "Leave it, Mick."

The discipline issue seemed to rally Ekland. "We can't desert our post. That was Captain Peabody's last order. But we should search the strong-room."

Hawkeye pointed out the practical problem. "Who has the key?"

It wasn't on the bunch still in the lieutenant's box-coat pocket. "Captain Peabody, he had it," Broome reported. "It was in the desk drawer, along with the office door key. I watched him take them out and hang them on his fob-chain yesterday."

"Is true," Wu agreed. "I saw it."

Hawkeye tried to think things through. "I don't rightly know the discipline of your forts, but it seems strange to me that your smith would make only one key for each door. What if that key was lost? Wouldn't your commander have one set put away safe, with another for everyday use?"

"I guess he would," conceded Rourke. "But we've not found any spares."

"Maybe they were on Major Bracewood when he left?" speculated Potter.

"Or was slaughtered," added McCrothy. "Wait... are you suggesting that the monster prowling the fort *has a set of keys?*"

Hawkeye tilted his head a little to acknowledge the possibility. "Suppose there's a place of concealment in the strong-room. A killer might hide there until nightfall, then let himself out with his key. He could prowl the fort's interior under cover of darkness while our watchers peer out into the dark forest beyond. He might place skulls where they'll strike fear into his enemies, or to lay sorcerous curses on his foes. When he finds a man alone, like Scargill sneaking to fetch you rum bottles from the storehouse, he might follow. A man alone in the storage hut might even call for help and not be heard. He might die there quickly and quietly."

Ekland shuddered. "Then what?"

"The attacker could carry the body back to his hiding place. After all, the killer has to eat."

McCrothy looked like he was going to sick up the jerky he'd had for supper.

"The leatherstocking might be right," Rourke considered. "How else would Captain Peabody be spirited from his office and a corpse be posed in his chair?"

"Unless it walked there," Wu offered unhelpfully. Potter cuffed him.

"We have to find the truth," Lt. Ekland decided. "We shall all go together. This is not the time to separate. Bring light and guns. We shall break open the strong room and..."

A gunshot boomed outside. Hawkeye recognized the sound of that carbine. "Uncas!"

He raced out of the mess.

"There was something down there," Hawkeye's brother reported. Uncas and young Clitheroe were both on the walkway above the fort gate, aiming their rifles down into the gloom of the compound. "Something moved, quietly and stealthily - like a man."

"Did you hit it?"

"I do not know."

Everyone assembled together. Rourke called for his soldiers to take burning brands and lanterns and look at the area where Uncas had seen a shadow. The Mohicans dropped down to the grass and inspected the area for tracks. The dried, pressed-down soil was not helpful.

"No sign of anything now," Potter proclaimed. "Nerves?"

"I saw something," Uncas insisted.

Hawkeye traced a bullet hole in the side of the chapel. "This is where your ball went." He prized out the squashed .45 caliber lead shot and inspected it. "No blood. You missed."

"Or the thing had no blood to spill," McCrothy feared.

"Potter, McCrothy, Broome, take watch on the walls," Rourke barked. "Clitheroe, it was you and Scargill what carried our pay-box into that there strong-room, wasn't it?

You come along and tell us if there's aught different there now. Hawkeye, Uncas, bring hatchets."

It was close to midnight and the night was getting chill. The whip-poor-whils made their mournful chorus, screeching their dole as if to call men's souls. Hawkeye and Uncas took axes to the strong-room door.

Ekland watched impassively, content to let his sergeant and the Indians take the initiative. Clitheroe stood guard with an unshouldered musket. The pigtailed Chinaman Wu made himself small in a corner, away from the gristly corpse that still occupied the commander's chair, but he cast frightened glances over at the butchered soldier.

Wu dà láng muttered something in his own language.

"What's that?" Sergeant Rourke snapped at him. "If you've something to say, speak up. In proper English."

"Stone knives, I said," the company cook answered, trembling. He pointed to Scargill. "The cuts there. Look. Ragged. Something sharp carved flesh, but not an iron blade."

Uncas examined the dead man. "He is right, brother. Flint?" he speculated. "Like the old tomahawks from ages past."

The lock on the strong-room door surrendered to the axe.

"Rifles ready," Rourke called. "Open that door."

Hawkeye eased the broken wood aside with his toe. The space beyond was little more than a cupboard sectioned off from the main office, no more than eight feet by ten. Two heavy metal pay-boxes stood side by side. Their keys were also lost with Captain Peabody and Major Bracewood. Like the rest of the administration cabin, the floor was timber, raised slightly from the hard turf it rested over.

"Bring light," Hawkeye told Uncas. When his brother held a lantern close, the scout began a minute search of the floorboards.

Ekland's nerves didn't hold out. "Well?" he asked.

Hawkeye's fingers traced an irregular groove where the planking ends joined. A square hatch would have been obvious, but one cut so that the panel was so eccentrically shaped could evade all but the closest inspection.

"There is a hole," the leatherstocking reported. "I'll open it. Stand ready."

Uncas and Clitheroe oriented their weapons. Hawkeye shouldered his own Kentucky rifle and pressed his hunting knife into the hatch's groove. The lid came up easily. It had been used recently.

A foul stench rose from the dark hole beneath – the rank odor of rotting flesh.

Hawkeye dropped a torch eight feet down. It landed on tunneled earth and revealed a low passage heading east, the shortest route to the fort's outer wall.

"Not a hiding place," Uncas realized. "A tunnel!"

Hawkeye lowered himself into the trench – and gasped.

"What?" demanded Ekland from above.

"I've found the missing men of Fort Woburn."

There they were, stacked like cordwood on either side of a burrow that must have taken months of painful labor to carve from the earth. There were dozens of bodies, all the missing redcoats, all butchered like Scargill for their meat. Many of them were missing their skulls, for those had been taken and boiled clean and bare as trophies and talismans.

Hawkeye had never felt so completely in the presence of evil.

And he was being watched. Watery yellow eyes reflected the torchlight. Something hunched and dangerous crouched in the shadows beyond the stacks of the dead.

Hawkeye fumbled for his pistol. The creature shifted. Something cracked, some old stick or bone. The roof of the tunnel began to fall.

"Out! Get me out!" Hawkeye called as the dead began to topple when the walls caved in.

Uncas' strong hands caught his shoulders and heaved. Hawkeye was dragged back through the hatch as the passageway and its charnel contents were buried in new rubble.

"What happened?" Rourke demanded. "What was it?"

"A trap," Hawkeye gasped. He coughed up as much of the corpse-dust as he could. "There was someone down there. Something. He'd rigged the tunnel to collapse."

Uncas braved a look down the hatch. "For certain there's no following that passageway now."

Hawkeye pointed east. "It heads that way, towards the soldiers' graveyard outside the wall. I think that must be where it comes out." He dragged out his water-flask and drained it dry. He still felt the dead in his throat.

"We'll search in the light," Ekland decided. "It would be suicide tonight." He stared at the collapsed tunnel with a worried look. "Who would spend so long carving such a secret way into this fort? And why?"

"Someone who hates you very much," Hawkeye judged. He described what he'd seen under the hut: the piles of gutted dead, the missing heads, the squat horror that had triggered the pitfall. "I still do not understand how all the men of the fort were taken, though," the scout confessed. "After all, one man might sneak from this tunnel by night, but from what we've seen a full fifty men or more were taken in daylight."

Mr. Wu stirred. "To cut up so many so quick is not work of one man," he argued. "These men die three day gone? It take long time to cut up ox or cow. Take as long with man, yes? One, he could not do all that in three day."

Clitheroe turned despairing eyes on his sergeant. "Sarge?"

"Yes, there might be more'n a few of 'em," the NCO agreed. "Working for the Frogs or just wicked on their own account."

Uncas remembered his father's words. "The ancient Misqas. The people of the mounds and tumuli. They tunneled. They used old weapons of stone and bone. They ate their enemies' flesh. But they are dead."

"Maybe," said Hawkeye. "If so, it's not stopping them."

Potter hefted his Brown Bessie musket at Rourke. "We're going," he warned this sergeant. "You can come with us or stay and die, but we're leaving now. Right now."

McCrothy supported his fellow mutineer with his own firearm. "That's right," the Irishman insisted. "This place is damned. Those murdered men's souls have been pinned here, stapled to their severed skulls to scream out all eternity. If we stay we'll be damned along with 'em!"

"Wait," urged Broome. "You can't just run into the night. What about the Misqas, or whatever it is out there?"

Potter spat. "What about 'em? It's no safer inside these walls. Ask Dan Scargill about that."

"Deserters swing," Lt Ekland warned. He looked pale and grim. He swayed a little as he tried to confront the mutineers.

Hawkeye and Uncas exchanged glances. Both of them had rifles slung at their backs, loaded pistols at their belts, but both were in Potter and McCrothy's line of fire.

"Deserters who have the silver from that pay-chest won't," Potter answered his officer. "They retire rich and men call 'em sir and scrape to 'em cause they're loaded." He gestured to Broome and Clitheroe. "Go haul them boxes out to the wagon again. Harness the team. Don't do anything else – we've got guns on the Sarge and our fine new lieutenant. And think yourselves, while you're getting our treasure, whether you'd not be smarter to cast your lot with us and get out of here.

Broome and Clitheroe hurried off to obey. Rourke glared at the deserters as if he'd like to rip their heads off and boil their skulls himself. "Damned cowards," he scorned them.

"There's a difference 'tween yellow and smart enough to know when to git," Potter insisted.

McCrothy turned his rifle directly on Hawkeye. "Tell us 'bout these Misqas redskins," he insisted. "What are they?"

"They are extinct," the scout answered, "or so it's said. When the white man came here there was war. The Misqas all died."

"Major Bracewood should not have pulled down the cairns," Uncas declared.

McCrothy crossed himself. He was sweating profusely, shivering in the bitter night. His musket-barrel shook.

Hawkeye continued. "If some of them survived, some inbred remnant that follows their ancient tradition, then desecrating their sacred mounds would sure bring 'em to war. Chingachgook said that this dead lake was special to them. Maybe that's why it's ringed with cairns of soapstones – or was, before Fort Woburn was raised here."

What else was raised by the redcoats' vandalism?

"Where are Broome and the boy?" demanded Potter. "They're taking too long."

Mr. Wu had slunk back as far as he could from the soldiers' guns. He had no illusions about how much Potter would enjoy shooting a Chinaman and two Redskins before he fled. Now he slumped to the ground, landing hard and not moving.

The rifles oriented on him. "What? What now?" demanded McCrothy.

"Get up!" demanded Potter. "Get up you slant-eyed yellow sonofabitch!"

Wu did not move.

Hawkeye glided over to the fallen Chinaman, careful not to make any move that the mutineers might consider hostile. He examined Wu dà láng where he lay.

Hawkeye found a pulse, thready but strong. The oriental was asleep!

Shaking didn't rouse him. "I don't know what's wrong with him," the leatherstocking admitted.

Potter kicked Wu in the ribs. "Get up!" he screamed. "Get up, you lazy bastard!"

Lt. Ekland also swayed and toppled to the floor.

"What is this?" Potter shouted. "What trick are you trying to pull?" he glared into the darkened parade yard. "Where's Broome with my money?"

McCrothy's nerve broke. "I'm getting' out of here," he told Potter. "I don't care about the silver. It's no use to a dead man." He hefted aside the big bar that sealed the fort's entrance and dragged one of the gates back.

He was impeded. Something was stapled between the two halves of the big door.

It was the headless corpse of Captain Peabody.

The officer had been fastened to the exterior of Fort Woburn's gates by screws taken from stores. Another of the stripped polished skulls was tied in place where his head should have been. As McCrothy tugged at the door the twine came loose and the skull clattered to the dirt.

The deserter screamed. He trembled all over, like a man with a falling fit. Then he fell insensate beside Lt. Ekland.

"No!" yelled Potter. He hammered his boot into his fallen comrade's side. "Get up! You can't leave me like this!"

Hawkeye moved. He leaped while Potter was distracted. He caught the end of the soldier's musket and pressed it upwards. When Potter instinctively squeezed the trigger, the smoothbore flintlock discharged harmlessly into the darkness.

Uncas came in too, grabbing Potter's arms in a half-nelson. Rourke caught on quickly and staggered in to assist, but he never made it. The sergeant faltered and fell before he reached the melee.

Potter struggled but his strength faded. His oath-filled cried slurred. His knees buckled. He was almost unconscious even before Hawkeye hit him.

Only Uncas and Hawkeye were left standing at the gate of the fort, where Peabody's headless remains prevented the doors from opening and a bleached skull gazed up at them with empty orbits.

Uncas looked over at his brother with wild eyes. "What black witchcraft is at work here?"

Chingachgook's white son didn't answer. Instead he threw his weight at the gate and heaved it shut again. He rammed the bar home. "The tunnel into the fort is sealed. They'll have to come over the walls."

"They?" Uncas asked. "The dead Misqas ghouls?"

"Whatever they are. They can't walk through walls, else why burrow a hole?"

"But they can make men fall asleep never to wake! That must be how they took the fort before. All those soldiers, lying helpless before the stone blades of their slayers!"

Hawkeye turned Wu's head so he could smell the Chinaman's breath. "There's a sour trace when he exhales." He checked Rourke and Ekland too.

"Poison?" Uncas guessed. "Then we too…"

"We didn't eat from the common pot, from the meat ration given all the soldiers. Wu wasn't fed from it either, but he's cook - if he helps himself to a portion he shouldn't take who'd know it? How if the intruder who haunted the fort by night laced provisions with some drug that sends men to sleep after a time?"

Uncas considered the idea. "That would explain why no food was raided from the store. They took the horses but the Misqas have no use for firearms or silver coin."

"They didn't need tainted beef and pork," Hawkeye said darkly. "They took what game they came from and slaughtered it for salting in that tunnel below."

Uncas shuddered. "If they believe we are all asleep they will come. Two rifles cannot hold this fort. What shall we do, brother?"

Hawkeye thought fast. "Broome and Clitheroe ate their ration. They must've fallen as they went to fetch the money. We should gather all the sleepers together so's we can protect them. We'll load them across horses and try to get away. There's nothing else we can try."

Uncas nodded. "Who will stay and watch these soldiers and who will hunt the others?"

Hawkeye knew his brother feared the Misqas but would not be found wanting. "I'll find Broome and Clitheroe, soon as we drag these men to the stable. Then you tether the team while I search."

Uncas nodded. The longstockings dragged McCrothy and Potter to the barn then returned for Ekland, Rourke, and Wu.

"Where shall we go?" Uncas worried. "The flood-waters have closed the river crossings."

"Away from here," Hawkeye replied. "Away from that black lake with its unrippled waters, and those endless mocking birds, and the high dolmens that seem to watch as men pass by. Away south. Anything's better'n here."

"Agreed," nodded Uncas. "If we can only…"

He fell silent as they dragged Rourke and Wu into the stable. McCrothy and Potter lay where they'd been left on the straw – but their heads were gone. Pungent welters of blood stained the hay crimson. The spray where their throats had been severed painted half of one wall.

Uncas lips moved the word, "How?" No sound emerged.

"You fired at a shadow in the yard, brother," Hawkeye remembered. "That was right before we inspected the admin office. Whatever creature you glimpsed didn't get chance to return through that tunnel and escape."

"He is still here!" gasped Uncas. "He must be close to us now!"

"Guard these men," Hawkeye commanded. "I'll fetch Lieutenant Ekland."

Uncas checked his pistol and stared around the gloomy stable. "Hurry," he told his brother.

Hawkeye hastened back to the gate. He half-expected to find James Ekland butchered too, but the officer still drowsed in his drugged stupor. The scout heaved Ekland over his shoulder and hastened back to the barn.

"What now?" Uncas breathed after they'd loaded the three remaining soldiers onto the carthorses.

"See to the animals. Stay vigilant. I'll seek Clitheroe and Broome."

"Be careful. Whatever is in this fort with us moves silently in the shadows and kills without hesitation."

Hawkeye nodded, swallowed, and slipped into the darkness.

Broome's throat had been gashed open with a rough sharp edge, severing his windpipe and slicing his jugular. Hawkeye found him in the passageway between the supplies hut and the barracks where he'd succumbed to the narcotic. He still twitched as the last life welled out of him.

The leatherstocking rushed forward but it was too late to save the man.

The Misqas dropped on Hawkeye from the roof.

The scout was alert for danger. He actually smelled the intruder – a sour stench of grave-rot and old fish – before the

Misqas landed on his back. Hawkeye had just enough time to shift his weight so that the assault spun him into the cabin wall instead of pinning him stunned to the floor.

The Misqas sliced at him with an obsidian knife. Hawkeye jerked back. The blade scored across his buckskin tunic, leaving a gash.

The Mohican rolled aside and came to his feet ready for combat. He got his first glimpse of the murderer of Fort Woburn. The Misqas was short and thin, all wiry muscle. He was naked save for a bone necklace and flesh armbands, but so covered in lake-mud and grease that his skin was black. In the dim light from the torches of the central green his eyes were yellow, glinting like a reptile's.

There was something wrong with the Misqas' mouth. It took Hawkeye a moment to realize that it had been widened by slitting the ends of the lips. Brown teeth were filed to canine points.

The leatherstocking tried to bring his long rifle round to take aim. The Misqas gave him no time, leaping forward with sharp-mailed hands for Hawkeye's throat. The scout fended the creature off with his gun-stock, but the intruder's wiry strength was greater than his compact body suggested. Hawkeye was toppled again, the Misqas straddling him. Sharp twisted fingernails sought his eyes.

Hawkeye used the length of his rifle to push the killer away. The Misqas wrestled him for the gun. The intruder's fingers were too short, joined at the first knuckle with webbed flaps.

"You want it? Fine!" Hawkeye growled, releasing his hold on the firearm. The Misqas jerked back, off-balance as the tug-of-war ended. Hawkeye drew his hunting knife and plunged it into the Misqas' side.

The killer made his first sound then, an inhuman screeching unlike any Hawkeye had heard from a man before. The wounded Misqas cast the firearm aside and hurled a ball of powder into the leatherstocking's face.

Hawkeye held his breath, but the dust got in his eyes. His vision blurred to uselessness. He was blind against this mortal foe!

But Hawkeye was a hunter. He relied on more than his sight to know where his prey lay. His other senses kicked in. His foe's rank pungency and the rattling of the finger-bones tied at the Misqas' throat were enough. Hawkeye's instinctive sense of how men moved – even this corpse-like demi-man – told him where to thrust. He brought his knife up and was rewarded as the blade made contact with something broad and heavy. Hot blood splashed across Hawkeye's fist.

The Misqas hit him hard, raking talons across the Mohican's cheek, slamming him down to the alley dirt. Hawkeye's blurred sight was full of livid will-o'-th-wisps, throbbing in time to the ache in his head. He slashed blindly with his knife to keep his enemy at bay.

A vicious blow sent the blade flying from his grip. Bony hands locked around his neck, finding the most vulnerable places to squeeze.

Hawkeye scrabbled at those thin corded wrists, trying to drag them loose. Breathing was impossible, and that grip was also impeding circulation to his brain. His clouded sight became darker.

I'm sorry, father, brother, he thought as the darkness took him.

He woke. He opened his eyes to a dim blur of light and shadow. A weight lay across him, pinning him down.

Hawkeye struggled up. His neck hurt. His cheek and side oozed where he'd been gashed by the Misqas. His buckskin leathers were soaked with blood. The bulk that pinned him was the intruder's corpse.

The leatherstocking pushed the dead killer away. As Hawkeye's vision cleared he could see the chest-wound that had ended the Misqas. His dying enemy had sought to drag him to death too. The Misqas had almost succeeded.

Hawkeye staggered to his feet. He retrieved his weapons and felt better for it. He stabbed the Misqas through the heart, to be sure. He checked that Private Broome was dead. He vomited.

When he'd got control of himself he returned to the fallen Indian and inspected him more carefully. The Misqas' fingernails and toenails were filled with the same kind of mud as that in the tunnel under the admin building. A leather pouch tied to one thigh contained strips of a meat that nothing in the world would induce Hawkeye to taste.

Under the mud covering, the Misqas was surprisingly pale. His proportions weren't quite right for a human being. His curved inbred frame seemed subtly wrong. Even touching that dead flesh made Hawkeye feel tainted.

That prompted another precaution. Hawkeye slipped into the supplies hut and found that forbidden liquor store. He broke open a bottle of strong spirits and washed out the scratches on his face and side. Better the sharp sting of cleansing alcohol than whatever taint the Misqas carried on his stone knife and nails.

Hawkeye didn't want to go outside again. He knew Uncas would be waiting anxiously for his return in the stable. He knew that young Private Clitheroe was still out there somewhere, fallen into stupor. The boy might yet be alive. But this night was not the hunter's friend. The darkness was inimical to mortal life. It was a Misqas moon.

Hawkeye checked his rifle's load and forced himself out into the darkness.

He found Clitheroe only a few steps away from dead Broome. The boy had been unable to drag his fallen comrade any further and had only made it round the corner before the drugs had dropped him too. Clitheroe breathed. Sometimes he twitched as if running in a nightmare.

Hawkeye hefted the lad over his shoulder and hastened back to Uncas.

"What shall we do, brother?" Uncas asked uncertainly as Clitheroe was tied across a horse like Ekland, Rourke, and Wu.

None of the options were good. "If it were just the two of us we might climb to the watchtower platform above the gate. Two good rifles might just hold off an assault 'till dawn. But we couldn't drag these four up the ladder."

"Could be lock them safe in the administration office?" ventured Uncas.

"They would not be safe."

"You killed the Misqas."

"I killed *a* Misqas. It took a whole lot of hands to claw out that tunnel and to skin them soldiers. How many more of those lost creatures wait in the forest? How many are scaling the fort's unwatched walls even now?"

Uncas shuddered. "Then we must take the horses and run for it. Let's get away from this cursed place."

"We need to get out of here," Hawkeye agreed. He wondered as he spoke if he was a coward for fleeing the fort. He wondered what his father would advise.

Uncas didn't have any such doubts. He checked the cords binding the sleeping soldiers and their cook to the four carthorses while Hawkeye saddled Peabody's and Ekland's riding mounts.

"We'll go back the way we came," Hawkeye decided. "At least we know the trail. Maybe we could swim the horses across the ford?"

"Anything is better than this place," Uncas replied.

Hawkeye made a last venture across the compound, to pick up essential supplies for the journey and to find Captain Peabody's map case. Then Uncas drew back the big bar on the gates and addressed the gory task of detaching the man that pinned them shut.

Hawkeye tucked his long rifle into the fold of his elbow and pioneered the way out. Uncas led the line of horses that carried the somnolent redcoats.

Hawkeye judged it must be three in the morning, near to the darkest hour. No star shone. A haunted sickle moon peeped intermittently through ragged high cloud, offering the only light. The night was bitter cold.

Uncas had padded the hoofs of the army horses to lead them as silently as possible. He watched behind while Hawkeye looked ahead. They took the track round the edge of the grey lake.

The first ripples they had ever seen on that still water glistened like broken mirror shards in the blue moonlight.

"Brother…!" breathed Uncas urgently.

Hawkeye saw it too - the motion beneath the lake's surface. When the first dark head broke above the waters he shattered it with a .45 ball from his carbine.

The Misqas rose from Lake Woburn. Hawkeye and Uncas did not know how the creatures had held their breath so long in that freezing liquid. They only saw the gaunt hunched remnants of that evil lost tribe rising towards them from the shallows: a dozen, then a score, then more, the people of the mounds and tumuli, the children of ancient sin, not yet fallen to final death. The Misqas clawed their way towards the escapees.

"Back to the fort!" Hawkeye cried. Fleeing these creatures was impossible now. This was their land, their night. A blind chase in the dark would be suicidal folly.

Uncas turned and spurred his mount for the gate. The other horses caught the stench of the beings slithering from the water and chased behind him in rising panic. Hawkeye brought up the rear, discharging his pistol and reloading in the saddle.

The Misqas moved wrong, as if their joints were different to those of normal men. They lumbered and crawled on all fours, but could dart with remarkable speed over short distances. That was how they brought down the tail horse in Uncas' chain, tumbling it squealing to the ground to be dragged along behind the stampede by its tether.

The next horse stumbled. Hawkeye rode in and cut the rope that tangled it to the rear animal. There was no other chance.

The Misqas fell upon the fallen horse and the man tied to it. They tore into Sergeant Rourke with a savage glee, shredding steed and soldier apart with those sharpened teeth, giggling as they ate.

A pair of the fastest Misqas leaped at Hawkeye's horse. The scout discharged his pistol at the first. The marauder fell beneath the horse's hoofs. The second managed to grab the strap of Hawkeye's saddle until the leatherstocking hacked the Misqas' hands with his hunting knife.

The terrified horse bolted again. It took all Hawkeye's strength and skill to turn the beast towards the gate of Fort Woburn. Eventually the frenzied mount got the idea and galloped the distance to the questionable refuge.

Uncas was inside. As soon as Hawkeye flew over the threshold, Uncas shouldered shut the heavy door and slammed the bolt back home. Mere moments later the gates rocked under the pressure of the Misqas that followed right behind.

"Rope!" Hawkeye shouted to his brother. "Fetch rope from the stable!"

An idea that had seemed impossible an hour ago was now their only chance. As the Misqas drummed at the entrance and sought to scale the stockade, Hawkeye and Uncas tied rope under the armpits of their three remaining charges and hoisted Ekland, Wu, and Clitheroe up the ladder to the guard platform over the main entrance.

Hawkeye judged this the most defensive element of the fort. The watchtower was protected on three sides from gunshot or arrows by a tall timber balustrade and by a sloped timber roof. It could only be approached from the ground by a long single ladder, or up short ladders from the walkways that ranged along the walls on either side. It had a good line of fire covering the gateway and approach, all the way down to the lake.

Uncas leaned over and fired a ball into one of the dark shapes battering at the doors below.

"Save your powder," Hawkeye told him. "We'll need it when they come over the walls and try to take us along those galleries."

Uncas saw his brother prepare to descend the ladder again and objected. "Where are you going? They might already be in the compound!"

"Chance I've gotta take," the leatherstocking answered. He remembered the words of the wandering preacher-man that Chingachgook had traded with to teach his sons their letters and numbers. "Needs must when the devil drives."

He dropped down into the Misqas darkness.

When Hawkeye returned, Uncas had rolled the three unconscious men against the front wall, where they were best covered from missile fire. Hawkeye handed up a jug of water, a half-dozen powder horns, a sack of ball, and a pair of spare rifles. "We'll need them," he judged.

The hammering on the gate ceased. Even the mocking trill of the whip-poor-wills died back.

Uncas pointed over the fort wall to the black lake. Something new was rising from it. She was pale and corpulent, naked like her kin, but bloated and vast. Her white hair was knotted with soapstone carvings. Her huge dugs were decorated with dead men's bones.

The Queen of the Misqas had come for the end.

From beneath the watchtower came the sound of the gate bolt being drawn back. The doors scraped open.

"They got in," said Uncas.

Hawkeye nodded grimly. It had only been a matter of time.

He glanced back at the corpse queen. She stood at the lake's edge, watching silently as her husbands and children ended the intrusion of invaders on her sacred soil. The fingernail moon painted her with shadow.

"They'll come now," Hawkeye predicted. "First an attack up the long ladder to distract us, then many of 'em along the walls. They'll count on us not being able to reload quick enough."

Uncas nodded. "If I fall…" be began.

"Then I will not be alive to send any message to our father," Hawkeye replied.

The brothers clasped hands and waited. They did not have to wait long.

The ladder trapdoor shook as it was struck from below. On the third blow the tip of a flint axe broke through the timber. Hawkeye pressed Lt Ekland's pistol to the rent and discharged it. The assault was stayed for a while.

Dark figures loped along the walkways from both sides.

"Here they come!" Uncas cried. "Too many!"

The last of the Mohicans was right. A rifle might take down the first. A spare gun could take the second. A belt-pistol would drop the third. But the fourth, the fifth, the sixth, all those who came after…

Hawkeye shouldered his Kentucky long-rifle and aimed in the darkness. If he had ever been true to his name then it had to be now.

He fired not at the incoming Misqas but at something he knew was there only from memory; something he had positioned during his final foray for supplies.

His ball struck true. It shattered the covered lantern beside the arsenal. Burning oil splashed down on the trail of black powder Hawkeye had laid to the barrels he'd dragged to the doorway.

The fort's gunpowder went up. The Misqas night boiled away in a blinding red flash. The Indians in the yard were sliced to pieces by exploding cabin or immolated in the fireball. Attackers on the wall were blown off, hurled over the stockade or blasted down into the courtyard. A triumphant plume of flame balled up inside the walls of the shattered fort.

Uncas and Hawkeye, crouched in cover atop the main gate, felt the whole structure shudder beneath them, but those charred timbers held.

The compound behind them burned. The invading Misqas burned with it.

Some few marauders still clung, confused, to the gallery around the stockade. To the west the stake-posts failed, dropping eighty feet of ribbon-wall into the inferno, taking men with it. Hawkeye and Uncas remorselessly fired again and again to the east where stunned Misqas still crawled, felling them like wounded birds.

Clouds scudded over the moon again, but the blaze of the fort lit the scene with a hellfire glow.

"Keep firing!" Hawkeye called. The Misqas before the gate milled around like cockroaches, exposed by the flames. The leatherstockings emptied load after load at them, exterminating them by raw instinct as a man might squash a venomous spider under his heel.

By the time the fires burned lower, leaving charred skeletons of huts beside burned carcasses of the barrows-men, the remainder of the Misqas had vanished. The night's chill pressed in again, sucking the heat from the fire. After the killing Hawkeye and Uncas began to shiver.

"Is it over?" Uncas ventured. He peered into the darkness towards the lake. "Have they gone?"

"Two hours till dawn," Hawkeye judged. "We better stay vigilant. There's something uncanny about these Misqas. They've been... touched... with something evil. Whatever they once were, they're twisted past reckoning now."

"They are dead souls," declared Uncas. "Is this what will become of the Mohicans one day? Of all the People?"

"It don't have to," insisted Hawkeye. "Whatever future awaits us, we don't have to become them."

Lieutenant Ekland groaned in his sleep, twitching at the visions that beset him.

Uncas listened to the night. The incessant nightjar calls had ceased when the fort had exploded, but some change in the atmosphere now alerted him.

"What is it?" Hawkeye asked.

Uncas cocked his head. "Something else," he replied. He peered over the tower at the gate below.

A fat white hand caught him by the throat.

She had climbed up the outside of the wall, that bloated Misqas Queen, clawing her way by driving ragged talons into the stockade wood. Now she shook Uncas like a kitten and hurled him away. The last of the Mohicans slammed against the watchtower's inner balcony rail then tumbled over it.

Uncas barely held to the edge of the tower, dangling thirty feet above the gate by one hand.

Hawkeye couldn't help him. The corpulent Misqas women slithered onto the platform, her bone-pierced breasts swaying to her belly, her chinless jaw lost in rolls of blubber as she hissed. She carried no weapon, but carved across her flesh in bloody streaks were ancient malefic runes. She seeped evil.

The scout raised his rifle, but she caught the end and twisted it from his hands. It clattered away, falling into the yard, discharging as it landed.

The Misqas Queen slapped Hawkeye, a backhand blow that set his head reeling. Her black talons reached out for his face.

Hawkeye scrabbled the flintlock from his belt and discharged it into the monster's bulging belly. The flesh split with a foul stench. Black blood oozed.

The woman ignored the wound. She caught Hawkeye by the hair and flung him the length of the platform. He landed hard and scarcely managed to roll aside before the Queen's corpulent flab dropped on him.

Hawkeye shimmied away. The obscene creature leered at him with watery yellow eyes, reptile eyes. Some primal memory, some ancient fear passed down through countless generations, warned the scout that he faced a foe that could rend his very spirit.

He reached to his belt, plucked knife and horn, and charged.

The mother of the Misqas swatted him as she might a fly. The longstocking's knife skittered away after his rifle and was lost. Hawkeye crashed down atop the insensate men he was trying to protect.

The Misqas Queen hissed in triumph and approached slowly.

Hawkeye's hand found Ekland's empty pistol. There was no time to load it.

And no need. Hawkeye only needed the flintlock. As the Misqas Queen overwhelmed him, he pressed the wheel right up to the open wound he'd made in her belly; the one where he'd jammed his powder horn during his last attack.

He sparked the gun.

The powder caught. The horn blew apart, spraying shards through the Misqas Queen's belly. The backlash seared Hawkeye's hands and eyebrows.

The Misqas Queen shrieked, then toppled. Her vast bulk clattered onto the boards, welling blood. Malevolent yellow eyes stared at Hawkeye until they finally froze in death.

Hawkeye felt her dragging his spirit with her, down to whatever hell she had chosen for herself and her people.

Only one thing saved him. He tore his gaze from that dead woman's stare and crawled over to pull his brother back to the platform. Hawkeye and Uncas lay side by side, gasping. Alive.

The Misqas were old and sullen, a remnant people who should have surrendered to death decades ago. Their queen was gone but their malevolence abided. They crept close in the darkness and waited for sufficient of them to take their revenge.

A slow grey dawn found almost a hundred of them squatting around the tower, brooding, biding their time.

With morning, the drug that had debilitated Ekland, Clitheroe, and Wu wore off. They woke from feverish dreams, pale, sick and unsettled, to find themselves living a nightmare. Hawkeye told them of the night before and of the danger they faced in the coming day.

"They're gathering their numbers and their courage," he warned the others. "We have little powder left now, and no more tricks."

The soldiers rolled the corpse of the vast pale Queen off the platform. She crashed down to the yard below and split open, disgorging black innards unlike anything the men had seen. Mud-smeared troglodytes of the Misqas crept in and bore her away to the lake.

"Now they will come," Uncas predicted.

A horn sounded to the west. A line of cavalry crested the tumulus hill. A standard-bearer lofted a British Union Flag.

The lead horse carried Chingachgook, returning for his sons. He had not traveled to Ipswich across impassable rivers but had instead trailed to the next fort in line and brought aid from there.

Some few Misqas scuttled away into the shadows, back to their ancient burrows to gnaw upon the bones of the dead, to suckle on the cold teats of their burst Queen, to worship their passionless gods. The rest seethed forward to meet the incomers, howling their hatred and bitterness, hungry for revenge and human flesh.

The cavalry mowed them down. The age of the Misqas had passed. The future belonged to the invaders and their technology, to logic and morality and organization and individuality – for now.

Ekland staggered down the ladder to welcome the relief to the remains of Fort Woburn. The stockade would never be repaired. "We held the line, sir," he reported to Captain Hammond, saluting.

"*You* held the line," Mr. Wu told Hawkeye and Uncas. "May your gods bless you for your deeds. May men always fight back the darkness."

"You did well, my sons," agreed Chingachgook when he heard what had happened. "Come, we will leave now. We do not want to be late to return to the Hudson."

"I will be glad to leave this place," Uncas confessed.

"And I," agreed Hawkeye.

Even as Lieutenant Ekland and Private Clitheroe explained to Captain Hammond what the leatherstockings had done, Hawkeye, Uncas and Chingachgook ghosted away across the lonely moors. They left the people of the mounds to their ancient hates.

About the Contributors

Jim Beard's work includes GOTHAM CITY 14 MILES, a book of essays on the 1966 Batman TV series; SGT. JANUS, SPIRIT-BREAKER and SGT. JANUS RETURNS, two collections of pulp ghost stories featuring his Edwardian occult detective; MONSTER EARTH, a giant monster anthology; and CAPTAIN ACTION: RIDDLE OF THE GLOWING MEN, the first pulp prose novel based on the classic 1960s action figure.

Currently, Jim provides regular content for Marvel.com, the official Marvel Comics website, is a regular columnist for Toledo Free Press and has forthcoming projects from Airship 27 and Pro Se Productions. Please visit him at http://sgtjanus.blogspot.com and on Facebook at http://facebook.com/thebeardjimbeard

Ron Fortier: A veteran comic book creator, he's best known for writing the Green Hornet and *Terminator: Burning Earth*, with Alex Ross, for Now Comics back in the 80s. Today, he keeps busy writing and editing new pulp anthologies and novels via his Airship 27 Productions, at: *http://robmdavis.com/Airship27Hangar/ airship27hangar.html.*

He won the Pulp Factory Award for Best Pulp Short Story of 2011 for "Vengeance Is Mine" which appeared in *The Avenger – Justice Inc.* from Moonstone Books and again in 2012 for "The Ghoul," which appeared in *Monster Aces*. He continues to write his own graphic novels and series, such a *Mr.Jigsaw Man of a Thousands Parts* via Redbud Studio. *http://www.robmdavis.com/RedbudStudio/index.html*

You can keep updated with his latest projects by visiting his personal website at *www.airship27.com*.

Van Allen Plexico is the award-winning and Amazon-best-selling author of a dozen pulp adventure novels in the superhero and space opera genres (notably the Sentinels series and the Shattering), along with more than two dozen short stories and novellas and five nonfiction books. Previous to this book he edited (or assistant-edited) and served as "show-runner" for GIDEON CAIN: DEMON HUNTER, SENTINELS: ALTERNATE VISIONS, BLACKTHORN: THUNDER ON MARS, all for White Rocket Books, and MARS McCOY: SPACE RANGER, Volumes One and Two, for Airship 27 Productions. Follow him on Facebook and on Twitter (@VanAllenPlexico) for the latest on his projects, as well as at www.plexico.net.

Frank Schildiner has been a pulp fan since a friend gave him a gift of Philip Jose Farmer's TARZAN ALIVE. Since that time he has published articles on Hellboy, the Frankenstein films, Dark Shadows and the television's Lovecraftian links. He is a regular contributor to the fictional series TALES OF THE SHADOWMEN and has been published in SECRET AGENT X Volumes 3 and 4 and RAVENWOOD, STEPSON OF MYSTERY, THE BLACK BAT MYSTERY by Airship27, THE NEW ADVENTURES OF THUNDER JIM and THE NEW ADVENTURES OF RICHARD KNIGHT by Pro Se Production and THE AVENGER: THE JUSTICE FILES by Moonstone.

His current projects include several more pulps, a book for Black Coat Press and a short story using his favorite Fletcher Hanks character, Stardust the Super Wizard. Frank works as a martial arts instructor at Amorosi's Mixed Martial Arts. He resides in New Jersey with his wife Gail, who is his top supporter.

I.A. Watson is a Redcoat from Yorkshire, England, author of award-nominated novels ROBIN HOOD: KING OF SHERWOOD, ROBIN HOOD: ARROW OF JUSTICE, ROBIN HOOD: FREEDOM'S OUTLAW, and BLACKTHORN: SPIRES OF MARS. All his publishers like colons. His short stories and novellas appear in lots of anthologies, including White Rocket's GIDEON CAIN: DEMON HUNTER, BLACKTHORN: THUNDER ON MARS, and SENTINELS: ALTERNATE VISIONS. He's won Best Short Pulp Story award once and been runner-up five times. There's a full list of his publications and some free stories at:
http://www.chillwater.org.uk/writing/iawatsonhome.htm
He is reasonably proficient with a bow and arrow but fumbles reloading a musket quickly when required to shoot the French.

Printed in Great Britain
by Amazon

75943939R00123